Mak

BELLE COATES

Parnassus Press Oakland California
Houghton Mifflin Company Boston 1981

Printed in the United States of America
S 10 9 8 7 6 5 4 3 2 1

A PARNASSUS PRESS BOOK

*The characters and incidents of this book
are fictitious and have no relation to any
person or happening in real life.*

Library of Congress Cataloging in Publication Data
Coates, Belle.
    Mak.
    Summary: An orphan of mixed heritage who considers
himself all Indian struggles to preserve Indian ways
while working with white men on his reservation in the
Montana badlands.
    [1. Indians of North America—Fiction.   2. Orphans—
Fiction]   I. Title.
PZ7.C628Mak   [Fic]   81-6533
ISBN 0-395-31603-0   AACR2

To Michael, Patrick, and Peter

Contents

1 Mak

Mak Malloy counted on his Indian-runner legs to get him to the school gate ahead of the others.

Actually, his legs were not all that much Indian. Three-quarters of the bone and muscle and speed of them was made up of sturdy white-man Irish. No matter at the moment. They got him there first.

Mak dropped his bead-tattered warbag at the gatepost, set his radio carefully on top, then turned to face the river bridge.

Any minute now Pop would drive across the bridge from Whitehorn with their summer supplies. Pick him up. Take him back to Halfway House in the reservation badlands. Back to Makosica.

Wasta! Good — that it was the first of June. Flower Moon. Except there were no wild flowers, with drought still pressing down like a heavy blanket all over the Montana river valley.

Again, no matter. For at last the Indian Boarding School was out for the summer.

At last he was going home.

Upperclassmen shot by with muffled yelps and thudding feet to join parents already waiting beyond the school gate in wagons and secondhand cars.

"S' long, Mak."

"S' long, Pete." Pete Light Thunder, his hay-farm pal. Joe Whip, captain of their basketball team. Molly Bear, from the mountain tribe, waving her roll of sketches. Moses Painter, son of their Council chief, puffing along in the rear.

Once off the school grounds and out of the principal's sight, Pete Light Thunder dropped his English and turned native. Right fist uplifted, Pete lowered it to his side in an arc, then opened it behind him in the sign of the closed hand, throwing Howard Granger away. Throwing all of Granger's tiresome government school away — the stuffy classrooms reeking of books and chalk, the deafening clang of machinery in the school powerhouse, the commands of teachers, the rules, the cod-liver oil and pitchers of milk that made them smell like fish and cows . . .

Mak clapped his mouth and let out a war whoop, sending Pete and the others on their way.

He watched them leap into rundown cars and wagons and rattle away toward the cabins and tepees that dotted their Montana reservation lands.

Mak probably wouldn't see his friends again until Moon of First Frost. He was left alone at the school gate in a pall of dust and heat.

For all his good run, he would be last to go.

Mak wheeled expectantly as he heard the throb of a motor. But it was not Pop's blue pickup. The motor belonged to a motorcycle that shot off the Agency road around the departing cars and wagons.

Mak watched the machine pitch and sputter over the rough stretch of ground between the school and the Indian Agency where the government employees lived. Its driver made a big show. Horses lunged in fright, wheels cramped, brakes screeched. Indian drivers yelled and shook their fists.

It had to be Les Bentarm on that motorcycle. No other Indian on the reservation was fitted out for such crazy wild-man riding.

After he showed his stuff, Les let his homebound tribesmen go on in peace, then swung his motorcycle toward the Boarding School gate. He stopped before Mak, pelting him with a scud of dust and gas fumes.

Les Bentarm wore thick leather boots and a hard white helmet. His dark face, greased with sweat, wore a different kind of hardness. He measured Mak from under the battered helmet — Mak's fair Irish skin and slanted, brown-streaked cowlick, his newly issued school shirt.

"Going back to Makosica to savvy up to white men, huh, Mak," he said over his wad of chewing gum.

Mak said, "I'm going back to help Pop sell gas and wait counter at Halfway House, same as always. Pop's late getting here, that's all. He must have got sidetracked loading up groceries."

"If he's gone off and left you, you'll be stuck with their crazy books and milk and rules till you hitch a ride."

Mak stiffened at the intended slur on Pop. "Pop said he'd be by."

Les pressed his point. "He's a white man, ain't he?"

Mak wasn't afraid of Les Bentarm. It just didn't pay to rile him. "Pop's one that keeps his word. He's been my pop since I was born almost. He's getting on now. He needs me to man the gas pumps and help Mary wait counter."

"Yeah, yeah. I've heard all that." Les switched his point. "What'll you be doing in your free time? You'll have a lot of that with trade dropping off on account of the drought."

Mak hadn't thought about trade in connection with the drought. Les Bentarm's talk only irritated him. He answered as though he'd dreamed of nothing else all spring. "In my free time, Les, I'll be riding all over Makosica. Raising alkali dust. Hunting stones and buffalo skulls to sell to tourists. Looking for my wa-sic . . ."

Les laid off for a moment. Wa-sic was some object found in nature — through danger — that channeled an Indian youth's own particular Life Spirit Power into making him a man. Wa-sic was a sacred, personal thing.

Les had a bear's claw working for him. Finally he said, "Watch how you point out Indian land to them tourists."

"They just look."

"That's what the first ones did. They just looked. Then they took — the best land us Indians had." Les Bentarm's brown eyes glazed over like marbles. "We can't be giving the whites ideas about taking any more Indian land," he warned, chewing away. "Or taking anything off it, either."

The slanted cowlick at Mak's crown bristled like a war feather. "What's getting into you, Les? White men don't want nothing in Makosica. Except maybe some stones and bones for souvenirs. They know our desertland's not worth anything. That's why they left it to us." Mak added levelly, "I'm Indian, same as you, Les."

"See you stay Indian, then. All Indian."

Les claimed to be a fullblood. He knew that Mak's mother had been a half-blooded river Indian, his father one of Pop's early-day Irish freighters. Les scorned every drop of the white man's blood that flowed in an Indian's veins. He said in parting, "There's some college guy staying at Barrack Ranch that's poking around in Makosica for souvenirs, too."

Mak stared after Les as he roared down the road toward the Indian Agency.

In some ways Les was smart. He'd graduated from the reservation Boarding School with honors. He tried cockily for a term at Whitehorn High across the river. Indian boys seldom attended the white man's school. Yet, in a switch, Les boasted he had a squaw-man uncle who was postmaster there. Even so, something went wrong. Les quit school. He'd find a job on the outside, he said. He was as good as any white. He knocked around trying for jobs in small towns, farms, factories. Looking . . . getting into trouble. He came back to the reservation with his motorcycle and a seething bitterness toward all white men.

Mak was too set on going home to try to figure out Les now. He jerked at the scratchy collar of his new school shirt.

Wasta wanitch! No good, Pop taking so long in White-horn when all the others had left an hour ago.

"You at the gate. Come here."

The sharp call broke into Mak's thoughts. He looked back toward the school grounds that he had left behind him.

Howard Granger, the sandy-headed school principal, leaned out of the front door of the boys' brick dormitory where he had his office. He motioned Mak to come.

Mak's heart gave a quick thump.

"What have I done now?" he asked himself.

Nothing bad, for sure. He'd guarded his actions well all year. No smoking or shirking work, no plotting to run away with other boys. Punishment at Granger's hands for such actions could be severe — even loss of a whole summer's vacation.

Mak shot an anxious glance toward the river bridge. If he left his post, Pop might think he'd got tired waiting and caught a ride with one of the mountain families driving through the badlands. If Pop went on without him, he could be stranded at school for another three or four days before hitchhiking a ride. As Les said.

Yet, if Pop came by while he was in Granger's office, surely he'd recognize the radio at the gatepost that he'd sent for Christmas.

In the school office Howard Granger folded a paper and thrust it into its envelope. He handed it across the desk to Mak.

"Don't lose this, Malloy," he cautioned. "Your grades

for the last two years are inside. You won't be coming back to this school anymore. Your foster father just phoned from Superintendent Stoner's office at the Agency that he has arranged for you to go away to a public school next fall. Away from Montana."

Mechanically Mak took the envelope. "Going where, did you say?"

Granger waved him off. "Mr. Williams will tell you all about it when he comes to pick you up."

Mak stood and stared.

"Close the door when you leave," Granger said. "I'm trying to keep it cool in here. And, Malloy."

Mak half-turned.

"I'll be expecting your new public school teacher to report to me that your grades have improved considerably over the last year. Hear?"

"I hear."

Mak returned to the school gate to wait for Pop. He stood beside his warbag and radio and stared numbly at the envelope in his hand.

Away to a new school, Granger said. Away from Makosica, land of his people. His foster father, Mr. Williams, would tell him all about it.

Mak's heart set up a beat like the slow rising pound of a war drum. The beat began to merge with another sound — the familiar throb of Pop's pickup coming down the road from the Agency. The sight of it, blurred like a mirage in the dust, gave Mak a feeling of panic, rather than the expected thrill of welcome.

He'd been set free from school only to find Pop cooking

7

up a deal in Superintendent Stoner's office to send him away. While he'd been waiting and worrying at the gate. He felt let down.

If only they had let him stay in Makosica, he would have found his wa-sic to hold him up.

Mary Sits, Pop's Indian cook, always said an Indian has to fight out his own problems. That's why he's still here today, Mary always said. Because he fights for his rights.

The pickup came on. Mak had another moment.

He turned and tossed Granger's report of his low grades over the fence behind him. He yanked off his new school shirt, sticky with sweat, and pitched it after the grades. Let Granger put it back in the commissary to issue to some other boy on some other last day of school.

Stripped except for jeans, his skin bare to breathe, Mak Malloy stood ready to face Pop Williams and find out about this business of leaving Makosica.

2 "I'm Glad I'm Indian"

"Hiyah, Mak."

"Hiyah, Pop."

John Williams was a man short on words. After nearly a year apart, he gave only a brief grin when Mak climbed in beside him. Then he stepped on the gas.

The old pickup swung away from the school gate. It settled itself solidly on the highway for the fifty-mile drive across the reservation plains to the badlands.

Mak studied Pop out of the corner of his eye, set to hear the worst.

Pop looked older, all dusty gray from mustache to shoetops. Forty years of life in the badlands country had saturated him with the dust of it. Even his voice was dry and dust-choked. He'd all but lost it with a tonsillectomy years ago in the Agency doctor's poorly staffed office.

Pop didn't mind getting along with only half a voice. He never had much to say, anyway.

Mak set his radio on the seat between them, then turned to toss his warbag into the bed of the truck.

"Hold it, Pop," he exclaimed. "You've got only two boxes of groceries back there. That won't hold us for the summer. You've left most of the supplies in Whitehorn."

If John Williams needed an opening he had it.

"I've got all we're going to need," he said, hunched stiffly over the steering wheel. "Three years of drought's cleaned me out. I'm leaving Halfway House. Going to California. Got a brother there."

The pickup climbed out of the narrow irrigated valley and headed through miles of seared range grass rooted in ground as hard as concrete. No sign of life around it, not even a bird. Only the quivering mirages of puddles that appeared to flood the highway farther ahead. When the panting pickup approached one of the pools, it disappeared to set itself on up the road. So that none of them

9

ever were reached. The work of evil spirits, come to torment and confuse . . .

Beside him the thread of Pop's tired, resigned voice tied the loose ends together.

"Time I retired, anyway. You're Indian and a ward of the government. I stopped by the Agency office and fixed it up with Stoner to take you with me. I promised him to put you in a good school down there."

A long speech for Pop. He figured it was all that needed to be said. He settled down to the business of driving.

Sure, Pop, he'd heard through moccasin telegraph during spring term about waterholes drying up, cattle dying, some white ranchers leaving the rim of the reservation. But the Indians had known other droughts. They came through somehow. And wasn't it always drought in Makosica?

Mak lifted his eyes from the mischievous game on the road to search the horizon. The badlands waited out there behind the wavering curtain of heat.

He was born in that hidden desertland. He carried the Indian name of it — Makosica. Mak for short.

Somewhere there lay his wa-sic, symbol of a personal power that would help preserve his Indianness. Without his wa-sic, far away in a white boys' school, he would grow into nothing but a shadow. A white shadow . . .

"California's an all right place to be, I guess," he said. "I hear about it on my radio. We studied about it at school. It's warm all year round, with tall trees — mostly tops — tall buildings, cars going every which way. All that. And an ocean besides. Maybe you'd like it there with your brother, Pop. But not me. I'm going to stay here on the reservation, in Makosica." He added, "It's because I'm Indian."

"You're only one-quarter Indian," John Williams said, looking straight ahead.

"Right," Mak agreed.

"I've brought you up as a white boy." Pop said.

That was only partly right. Mary Sits had had a hand in it, too. Mary never let him forget he was Indian.

"You could pass for white anywhere," Pop said.

Mak had only to stand before a mirror to know this was true. His skin was divided between dark and fair, his hair divided between brown and black. The blue of eyes inherited from his Irish father were blended to hazel by flecks of brown from the darker eyes of his Indian mother. But deep inside, where no mirror could reach, Mak knew he was all Indian.

His foster father didn't realize that. He gave him bed and board, tended his boy needs — made him brush his teeth, get up, get to work, change his jeans. But Pop didn't know him inside because he himself was not Indian.

Actually, John Williams never had much to do with Indians. For forty years he'd lived on Indian land leased for a freighter and tourist stop. Made out all right for himself, too. But Pop did business with white men. Sure, he gave handouts to hungry Indians now and then, a few gallons of free gas, but he lived apart from them as a people. Mak never thought to hold that against Pop. Now, suddenly, he was torn by the breach of race in their closeness.

Pride in his Indian ancestry carried Mak on over the hurt. "I don't want to pass for white, Pop. I want to stay Indian, the way I was born. I'm glad I'm Indian."

11

"Where will you live if you stay?"

"I can get along at Halfway House by myself."

"I owe the Indian Tribal Council for two years' lease money on Halfway House, on account of the drought," the older man countered over the steering wheel. "I've had to turn the buildings over to the Council. The Indians plan to wreck the place for the lumber and firewood."

Mak was like a wild colt that refused to be headed off. "I've got a hideout in the banks of the coulee — with a spring way back. I can shoot jackrabbits, pick buffalo berries. I'll find my wa-sic — " He broke off, angry that he'd been sent off to the Boarding School so he couldn't search Makosica for his power.

"Wa-sic!" Pop snorted. "You've let Mary fill your head with a lot of superstitious nonsense. I'm not about to leave a kid of mine to shift for himself in that godforsaken wasteland. It's good for nothing, except to hide out cattle rustlers and bank robbers and half-baked gopher-hole miners."

Pop was forgetting he'd made a good enough living in that same "godforsaken wasteland" before he let a few dry years scare him out.

"Even white ranchers like George Barrack can't make a go of it in this drought," Williams went on. "Barrack's getting out. He's trying for a service station job in Whitehorn. Move his family there until the drought's over."

A spell of coughing choked Pop off. Mak remembered Gail Barrack galloping her paint pony along the rim of the badlands. Her yellow dog raced before her. Her yellow hair streamed behind. Sometimes she stopped at Halfway House to buy beadwork of Mary Sits, and to have a friendly word with him.

Throat cleared, Pop began pecking away once more at the shell of Mak's determination. "You belong in a school with white kids your own age. Go-getter young folks like Jim Barrack and his sister. Fit yourself for a job in the white man's world. Like your dad. Better'n your dad."

"All I'll ever want is the Makosica, Pop. I plan to stay right here — no matter what else there is."

John Williams began a final rasping protest that ended in a squeak. He'd lost his aging voice in the hot dry wind.

They drove on in silence. The shrouded shapes of pinnacles and tablelands in Makosica began to advance their natural contours out of the blanket of heat. Pinky's Thumb . . . Heaven Hill . . . Ghost Ridge . . . Big Bench . . .

Mak knew them all as he knew the palm of his hand. His eyes held to these things he knew as the pickup brought them closer.

The dusty blue pickup slid over the edge of the reservation plains and down to the ovenlike floor of the great desert basin. John Williams commanded the last shred of his spent voice in a final plea to hold them together.

"I won't be around always, Mak. I've raised you to know what's right and best so as you can choose for yourself when the time comes. There's no decent job around the reservation for a smart young Indian like you. Indian boys who want to amount to anything get away from here to live and work in places outside. Like Joseph Blackstone."

Joseph was Mary Sits' nephew. He was working his way through some college back East. Mak had almost forgotten about Joseph.

Some of them were coming back, though. Jim Cloud, Serena Mann, Les Bentarm.

Only last week some of the upper-grade boys had gotten up nerve to ask Les what it was like on the outside.

Les told them, his eyes hard as marbles beneath his dented white helmet. "Okay. You start out to make good in this white man's city. See? You try hard as hell to get used to things. But you can't talk with nobody. Or get a job. Or find your place. You go hungry. Get sick. Finally everything breaks loose inside you. You take a swing at some smart white guys. You get beat up for a no-good Injun and left in a gutter. That's what it's like."

Les had streaked away on his motorcycle like a wild puma snarling at a bullet in its side.

No use wearing out Pop's voice with arguing. Mak didn't want to try it on the outside. He wanted to stay in the land of his mother's people.

He didn't know how he'd make it — with Pop beside him in the pickup and already a thousand miles away.

Maybe Mary Sits —

3 "Go Find Your Wa-sic"

Then he was home again. At Halfway House.

Pop drove through the barbed-wire gate, thrown open and left to rust in snarls at its posts. Bent and stiff-legged, he crossed the sun-baked dooryard for the wash house and left Mak to carry in the groceries.

Mary Sits' mongrel dog lifted himself from the shade of the house to bark a languid welcome. Nite Boy's nicker joined in from the direction of the corral. The animal chorus gave Mak a sickening sense of loss, like the wail of an Indian death chant.

He remained in the pickup, holding to the side of the seat, holding to himself. He stared at the low, dun-colored building, part log, part added-on clapboard, that squatted before him.

Rooted firmly in hardpan, Halfway House had stood up to forty years of blizzards and windstorms and the blaze of desert suns. It had sheltered an army of freighters who stopped for food and rest. Rough, tough-muscled men who called him Mac, wrestled him, and gave him gum and pennies. Mike Malloy, the father he never knew, had slept beneath its roof.

Now, under the hand of drought, his old home seemed dwarfed and shriveled beneath the towering peaks and bench lands. Mak's throat ached just to look at it.

He turned to stare instead at the gas pumps before the

house, dust-eroded and deserted of customers. That didn't help him to feel any better. Only to remember . . .

A year ago he had hustled between the shining tanks and the lunch counter, giving service to truckers and information to tourists who began to trickle through on the new highway. He could answer any question they put to him. He knew Makosica better than anyone around.

Makosica? It meant badlands. *Mako* for land. *Sica* for bad. Not that the land itself was bad, he always hastened to add. Only that it was bad to travel through.

The Drinking Cup? Once it was a big lake. Then it swallowed a herd of stampeding buffalo and turned into a slough of quicksand. Evil spirits bubbled there now to suck at men's feet.

That sweet smell came from Indian musk. To get yourself a bunch of it, take the cutoff through Scorpion Flats to Heaven Hill. Only, stay in your car on the Flats. Those scorpions had poison in their bites.

Not safe for newcomers to poke around in Makosica. But if the desert draws you, then stay away from the canyon below Big Bench with the Spirit Face carved on its wall. That was the face of one of the spirits who turned good Indian grasslands into badlands. It was left behind as a reminder of spirit power. Not even the boldest Indian ever went near that spot.

He sent the sightseers on their way with the sign for goodbye and good will.

Right hand horizontal to his heart, he swept it out to join his left hand in front of his face. Throwing out both hands, palms up, he made a grand sweeping curve even with his shoulder.

16

Smart salute and Indian ritual in one, it held the power to color the grotesque crumbling domes and yawning chasms into a picture-book fantasy for the uneasy travelers. It left them with another kind of wonder about the kid back there who talked like an Indian but looked like a white boy.

Now it was a different summer. His old home, stripped and empty, stared back at him with half-closed eyes, awaiting the wrecker's ax.

And he had no wa-sic to help him find another.

Mary Sits chewed coffee beans instead of gum. When she turned from the kitchen cookstove, Mak caught the familiar scent of coffee on her breath. And he knew he was home.

He set the cartons of groceries on the table. For a long moment they looked at one another above her smoking skillet, Indians together.

She was heavy and middle-aged plain in her braids and dark blue percale and moccasins. Her sharp brown eyes swept over him, noting the absence of the customary school shirt. At the same time she made it seem a long way up the height of him to the bristle of his cowlick.

Mary made no mention of the empty gas pumps, the vacant lunch counter, Pop's planned desertion. She waited for Mak to speak first.

How much could he count on Mary to help him? He had told Pop he could take care of himself. Yet, it was different with Mary. She was of his race, matron of his tribe. She sat on the Tribal Council with nine men. Young and old came to her for advice. She had helped to raise him.

When he had been orphaned and left at Halfway House after the blizzard, Mary had carried him all over Makosica on her blanketed back, telling him legends of the desert creatures, eagle, coyote, rattlesnake, with Moon and Father Sun above. When he could walk she had sent him across the lonely wastes to find porcupine quills to weave into her beadwork.

When he had reached his teens she'd named him for their land — Makosica Mike Malloy. She had made the land a part of the blood and bone of him.

Mary was full of contradictions, too.

Once in fondness he had called her Mother and she had denied him. "Makosica, the Earth, is your mother," she had said fiercely.

"Be proud you are Indian," she had exhorted him. Then she cut off his braids so Pop could send him from Makosica to the Boarding School on the river and learn to live like a white boy.

Herself a graduate of the Boarding School, Mary had taken a job as cook at John Williams' Halfway House and had saved her wages in the Whitehorn Bank like any thrifty white girl. Yet, she refused to sleep or eat at Halfway House. She cooked her meals over a campfire outside her tepee on the rim of the coulee. Her sunrise prayer song had floated over Makosica to waken Mak each morning for as long as he could remember. In the kitchen she had laughed with him over the funnies.

From her he had learned the origins of their people. "We are Earth People," she had said. "Our ancestors came out of a passage beneath the earth. Our children have remembered, so the legends are not lost. The records lie in

18

our land for those who will look."

Records like the faint Indian pictures carved on the wall of his cave hideout in the coulee below Halfway House.

Mary had nagged him to find arrowheads to sell to tourists, but when he had brought the strange, long arrowheads from under the ancient recordings on the wall, she had given him an uneasy push and had made him take them back as sacred from the past and not to be disturbed.

Standing before her now in the kitchen at Halfway House, Mak was reminded of her most confusing contradiction of all. It had to do with the treasured headdress that she kept in a box in the back of her tepee.

Mary had inherited the headdress from her great-grandfather, Chief Earth Boy. Its long rich train of eagle feathers, adorned with weasel tails and banded with beads, must have swept to the very heels of the giant chieftain.

Her stories of Earth Boy's hunts and wars, the traditional dances and feast days he presided over, had filled Mak with awe and native pride.

"Earth Boy was great," Mary had said proudly, "because he could see far with his brain as well as with his eyes. And he knew when it was time to change."

Change? How? What did Mary mean by extolling the great Earth Boy as a symbol of change while she filled Mak with beliefs and legends of their people that never changed? Her use of the word irritated Mak because he did not intend to change.

He said in the Indian tongue, "I am not going away with Pop."

He thought he caught a flicker of relief in her eyes. "Where then?"

"I don't know — yet." With you, he wanted to say.

She shook her head as if he had spoken, and told him in sign that she meant to live at her sister's cabin near Antelope on the east rim of Makosica. It was poor and small, already crowded with a big family. Mak knew it would be the same at the homes of any of their friends. All were cramped, filled with hunger during the drought.

"I'll find my place, somewhere here in Makosica," he said, his head high.

"Foolish talk," she scolded him, as had Pop. "You be only a boy. You can't make out here alone."

He stared at her with accusing eyes. She had taught him to be Indian — an Indian fights out his own problems; that's why he's still here today. Now she denied him the right to fight for his place as Indian.

What then, wise woman of my tribe? California with Pop?

Mary was ready for his unspoken question. He knew, even before she answered, that he had the answer himself. The way to find his place in Makosica was the way to find himself as Indian.

She put him on his own and challenged him above the smoking skillet.

"Go find your wa-sic."

4 Shungatoga Lost

Lips dripping, Mak's black pony drew back from the watering tub in the pole corral, ready for Mak to mount. The bulging canvas waterbag hung from the pommel of the saddle. A coil of rope hung on the opposite side.

It was barely sunrise, yet already the burn of sun was on Mak's bare back, the fine sand, borne on the shifting wind, gritty in his teeth.

He grasped the stirrup, turned it, then hesitated. He didn't know what lay ahead, or when, if ever, he'd return. Beyond the seat of the saddle, he could see Mary Sits beading at the entrance of her leaf arbor on the bank of the coulee above the corral.

The leaf arbor, built of cottonwood branches driven into the ground and laced together at the top, formed a dome that cooled the hot wind as it sifted through the leaves.

Old Cloud Rise came early from across the reservation to sit cross-legged before the arbor's entrance. Something disturbed him. His arms and dark hands moved vehemently in sign.

Mary paid him attention while she worked, also aware, Mak felt, that he was delaying his departure from the corral below.

21

Easy enough for Mary to say, go find your wa-sic. A young Indian couldn't just go out and pick up any trivial thing and call it wa-sic. Wa-sic must hold personal meaning. It must come at the right time, through struggle in the face of danger. Only then would it have power to guide and protect its finder in the way he chose to go.

His Life Power would have to be exceptionally strong to help him find a home in the badlands country where Pop would be willing to leave him. Mary Sits, beading in her leaf arbor, knew that.

She knew he had searched other summers and returned empty-handed. She knew he stood at his stirrup now, undecided, dreading to set out for fear of returning empty-handed again.

Already Pop was packing their bags in the back bedroom. Tomorrow Mary would gather up her tepee, her precious chieftain's headdress, take her mongrel dog, and go live with her sister at Antelope.

With no home and no power to find another — and with Superintendent Stoner in agreement — there would be nothing for him but to leave for California with Pop. That is, unless he chose to run away and lose himelf forever in Makosica.

All through the night he had laid plans for that very thing. Pop and Mary had said he could not exist alone in the fierce, barren emptiness of Makosica. For all his big talk, his secret plans, they were right . . .

A shadow fell on the hot hard ground before him. Cloud Rise had come down from Mary's leaf arbor to speak with him.

The old Indian wore dark glasses and a loose shirt over faded trousers. He carried a bent cottonwood stick for a cane.

"How." He greeted Mak with the sign of the lifted open hand. It was the universal sign of friendship among plains Indians; it showed that no weapon was carried.

"The drought takes my white horse, Shungatoga, to Big Bench in Makosica for grass," Cloud Rise informed Mak in signs. "Spirit Face that grins from the canyon wall below Big Bench won't let me go there to get him. My wa-sic is strong, but not strong enough against that evil spirit. Your power, Makosica Mike, takes you safely all over Makosica. I want you to ride out there and bring my Shungatoga back to me."

Mak started to tell the anxious old Indian that he had no wa-sic. That he, too, always kept a safe distance from the canyon with the grinning Spirit Face upon its wall.

He stopped short to glance sideways toward Mary Sits, bent like a half-moon over her beadwork. And seemingly as far away. Had Mary sent Cloud Rise to him with this fearful errand? A search for a lost horse on Big Bench, so near to Spirit Face, could be dangerous.

It could be his last chance to find his wa-sic . . .

A trembling began inside Mak that came from an angry determination of his own.

He threw his soul into a prayer to the Great Spirit for a sign that he would be protected. Then he swung into the saddle.

"I'll go find your Shungatoga, Cloud Rise."

He rode off into Makosica without a backward glance.

The immense, sparsely grassed plateau called Big Bench reached its parched palm into the badlands from out of the rangelands on the south rim. Cooled somewhat by the canyons that ringed its base, grasses there were less scorched by drought than on the mainland.

Best chance of spotting Cloud Rise's lost horse on Big Bench would be from the top of Pinky's Thumb, the highest peak around. The great bent column of pinkish rock beckoned Mak, thumblike, from out of shimmering white stretches of alkali flats.

As Mak rode toward it, a rider on a paint pony emerged along the plains road a mile beyond him. It was the girl from Barrack Ranch with her yellow dog racing ahead, her yellow hair streaming in the hot wind.

Gail Barrack caught sight of Mak on the floor of the badlands below her. She lifted her arm and waved.

Mak waved in return. No use for Gail to stop at Halfway House to buy any more beadwork, he could have told her. The display stands were empty of beadwork now, along with the "junk," so-called by Pop, that he'd picked up in Makosica as souvenirs to sell to tourists. Buffalo skulls and snake rattles and arrowheads, horns and softly tinted stones — some with strange shell-like markings that brought high prices.

It pleased him that the ranch girl liked Indian beadwork. He wondered what she did with so much of it. Anyway, soon she and her parents and brother Jim would be gone from their ranch home to live in Whitehorn. He'd miss seeing her and her paint and her yellow dog.

Mak ground-tied Nite Boy at the base of Pinky's Thumb. Spiral fashion, he began to climb the great bent rocky column. He dug in his toes, watching for thorns on scrubby bushes that he clutched for support, keeping an eye out for loosened stones and hidden rattlers.

Finally he stood at the tip of the great Pinky's Thumb. The grotesque panorama of the badlands opened up beneath him.

The Barrack girl, Pop packing bags in his bedroom, Mary beading in her leaf arbor, receded from his thoughts.

As always, he stood spellbound before the savage grandeur in the welter of peaks and canyons at his feet. Wind and rain had made flowing shapes from sandstone — giant toadstools, fangs, scallops. Frost had split pillars into wafers, piled like plates. Mak knew these muted formations, the mile-high benches and knife-edged ridges, as he never could know beaches and palm trees and freeways. His Indianness was tied up in them. The silent loneliness, the mystery and danger, excited and fortified him. The vast dusty flats and eroded buttresses, chalklike against the burning sky, gave him a sense of dignity.

Makosica had not always been a wasteland of rocky peaks and barren flats. According to Mary Sits, it once was a fine grassland and hunting ground like the plains surrounding it.

"Then a fierce mountain tribe came to drive us away," she told him. "For years we tried to appease the spirits with fasting, dances, even with torture, to get our homeland back. Finally the spirits answered. They killed the enemy by striking the land with lightning and fire and giant earth upheavals. Our people returned. But they found their grassland torn into strange shapes of rock and flats that grew nothing but cactus and tumbleweed and rattlesnakes. The wild game was gone. There was no rain. Only the angry Father Sun. To remind us of their great power, the spirits left one of their faces on the canyon wall below Big Bench."

The Indians could not ranch or farm in their barren desertland. They retreated to the bordering plains to cluster on the rim of its destruction.

As he looked out upon it from the tip of Pinky's Thumb, Mak wondered if the spirits had formed that great wasteland for some other reason than just to kill an enemy. Could they have hidden something of worth beneath its worthlessness? The legend didn't say so.

And today there were other things to think about.

His keen hazel eyes swept the long flat top of Big Bench three or four miles beyond him. He caught a swift, flowing movement there. Horses running. But the lead horse was dark, not white like Shungatoga. Mak recognized him as the wild appaloosa stallion that inhabited Big Bench.

The mustang stallion turned swiftly and led his harem of fleet dun-colored mares out of sight into a hidden gully.

"He's caught wind of me," Mak thought to himself.

He'd need strong wa-sic to catch that one. Maybe some day he'd have the power to try.

Mak sighed. Need for his wa-sic weighed still more heavily upon him.

Then his probing eyes caught a faint moving dot of white among the scattering of rocks and brush along the near edge of Big Bench, the featherlike swish of a tail.

"That's him — Cloud Rise's horse," he exclaimed aloud.

To the right of the grazing horse and below it, Mak located the shadowy line of canyons that emptied into a gorge at the foot of the Bench. One of those canyons held the dreadful Spirit Face upon its rocky wall. Mak felt his heart quicken at the thought.

No matter, really. The white horse stood at the near point of the Bench, high above and this side of the line of canyons. Mak figured he could reach the Bench at its near end, rope Shungatoga, and leave within an hour without invading the canyons.

Bare ground exposed to sun can turn warm breezes into fiery blasts. Mak and his tough little pony were exhausted with heat by the time they had crossed the last of the alkali flats and reached the base of Big Bench. In his haste to capture the lost horse, Mak had crowded out the need to spare himself or his pony. Even the need to find his wa-sic was put from his mind.

He left his pony in the shade of a giant boulder at the base of the Bench, and started the climb on foot. To climb it on Nite Boy, thrashing about for a footing in the loose shale embankment, might start an earth slide. It could engulf both of them under tons of soil and stones.

With the loop of rope swinging from his belt as he climbed, Mak made plans. He would slip up on the grazing horse from behind the boulders that lined the rim, and rope him from the ground. Shungatoga was an old horse and fairly gentle. It should be easy.

He reached the top of the Bench and looked about in the blazing sunshine. Cloud Rise's horse no longer grazed in the open area along the rim. He was not among the nearby clutter of rocks and small boulders.

Impossible in so short a time, yet Shungatoga seemed to have vanished completely from the top of Big Bench.

5 Indian Against Himself

"Shungatoga's gone down over the rim," Mak concluded to himself. "Probably looking for a spring in the gorge."

He hurried to check the steep slope of the embankment at the west side of the Bench.

No tracks leading to the rim. No sign of an animal slide in the loose shale of the bank. No sign, either, of the horse in the bottom of the gorge that cut into the floor of the badlands immediately below Big Bench.

It was as though Cloud Rise's white horse never had been anywhere near Big Bench.

Determined not to let frustration get the better of him, Mak began to search the interior of the great desert plateau. He hurried across a carpet of crisp, curly buffalo grass, threaded through scattered rocks and clumps of cactus and sage. He looked from left to right. He could find no trace of Shungatoga anywhere on the surface of the Bench.

The desert sun poured over him like liquid fire. His steps began to drag. His thinking dulled.

"The white spot I saw from Pinky's Thumb must have been a rock," he decided. "It just looked like a white horse through the heat waves."

But he had seen the animal move, saw the sun-screened flick of tail.

He longed for a drink from his waterbag hanging on his saddle below the point of Big Bench. Yet, he would not leave his search.

If only there was a boulder large enough among the scattering of rocks to offer shade and rest for a moment. Under the silent fiery pressure of the sun he moved without direction. He communed with himself. He began to argue back and forth, as if torn apart into two beings, the way his blood was divided into two races. Like two brothers turned against one another.

"Give up the search. The horse isn't here."

"I saw him. I gave Cloud Rise my word to bring him back."

"Evil spirits have taken him. Your word can't win against them."

"I'll find my wa-sic to help me get him back."

"Haven't you searched wa-sic for years and never found it? Be smart. Go live an easier life with Pop. You don't have to turn out like Les Bentarm and those others."

Conflicting thoughts swung at him like war clubs, splitting his head with pain. He blundered aimlessly along in his search.

Finally a whole way of life as he knew it became blotted out of his mind.

He turned back and stumbled toward the point of the Bench, intending to descend it to reach Nite Boy, tied at the boulder below. Have his drink. Get away from the wrenching division within himself, the torturous grip of the sun. Go back to good old Pop, packing their bags in the bedroom . . . To swim in cool ocean waters and rest in the shade of palm trees . . . To whiz along freeways with the cool ocean wind whisking away his troubles . . .

Mak reached the rim of Big Bench sooner than he expected. Blinking uncertainly, he stared down the steep shale incline into the furnace of white heat that rose off the alkali flats. His aching eyes tried to locate the shaded boulder where he had left Nite Boy and the waterbag.

Finally he realized that he hadn't reached the point of the Bench after all. He stood instead at the western side of it.

As he turned away, a movement below him arrested his eyes. Cloud Rise's horse appeared out of the glaring whiteness on the rim of the gorge immediately below Big Bench.

Shungatoga caught sight of Mak and threw up his head with a snort.

How could this be? The white horse hadn't been there seconds ago.

This was no ghost horse. Real, almost playful, Shungatoga turned about and began to move with quick steps into the bottom of the gorge.

He looked back, as if daring Mak to follow him to the rock-strewn floor, then headed nimbly for the mouth of a canyon that angled into the gorge on his left.

Simple enough, Mak reasoned. Grown thirsty, Shungatoga had come down from the Bench through some route unknown to man to find a spring in the canyon.

Yet, not so simple.

As the thirsty horse headed directly up the floor of the canyon, Mak saw from his higher position that there was another canyon emptying in the gorge, and farther on, still a third.

The third canyon along the base of Big Bench held the dreaded Spirit Face embedded in its wall.

Mak never had seen Spirit Face, but legend told him exactly where it was placed. In his confusion and blundering haste he had forgotten. He was unable to identify the face from where he stood because it was set far up in the canyon and hidden by its walls.

Shungatoga moved in compulsive haste in the direction of the third canyon. He seemed drawn by some power other than thirst. A strong, unseen power, which was pulling at him.

Anger came to sharpen Mak's dulled senses.

This was the work of Spirit Face. Its evil power had reached out from the canyon wall to make game of the horse. It had caused Shungatoga to disappear from the Bench, then to reappear below it. Now it caused the animal to flee toward it so that his pursuer must follow there in order to rope him.

The power of Spirit Face was making game of him, the

Indian, also. Numbing him, setting him against himself, luring him toward disaster. Tricked by its fearful spell, the entire course of his life could be changed.

How could he expect to break the spell of that evil spirit?

Voices came from outside himself, yet were a part of the whole of him. A scraggly voice . . . and the silent voice of sign . . .

Know what is right and best, then choose for yourself.

Fight out your own problems. That's why you, an Indian, are here today . . .

Mak stood on the west rim of Big Bench, clenched his right fist, and lifted it high. Then he swung it down in a swift arc past his side. He opened his fist behind him in the sign of the closed hand. He threw away the part of himself that Spirit Face had weakened and divided.

He plunged down the side of the bluff toward Cloud Rise's fast-disappearing white horse, determined to rope Shungatoga before the power of Spirit Face pulled him any closer.

He'd have to hurry.

6 Wa-sic

Mak leaped and slid and tumbled down the loose shale of the embankment. Bruised and coated with dust, he picked himself up at the base of Big Bench and hurried to overtake the fleeing horse.

There was not time to reach Nite Boy and ride him in the chase. Flashes of white mane and tail told Mak that Shungatoga was rapidly losing himself among the turns and rocky obstructions of the first canyon.

Moments later he caught sight of the horse near the wall of the canyon. Mak loosened the rope at his belt in readiness for the throw.

Shungatoga caught the movement of Mak's hands. He leaped a washout — scoured by rare and violent rains — and switched his course to the opposite wall, where he disappeared around a pile of boulders.

The boulders were hot and close together, their edges sharp. When Mak climbed across them, he found that he had reached a fork in the canyon.

Shungatoga was nowhere in sight. Which way had he gone, to the left or to the right? The way to the right looked less steep, less rocky. The horse must have taken the easier passage. Mak chose the right fork.

Except for a rough pebbly bottom, the way up the canyon was clear. The only boulders in the narrow area were close to the banks, none of them large enough for the animal to hide behind. The rocky sides of the canyon were too steep for a horse to climb. Mak broke into a run.

Then, at a turn in the canyon, he was confronted by a dead-end embankment that blocked his way with heaps of loose rock, brush, and gravel.

He had chosen the wrong fork. Shungatoga had been drawn into the more difficult route, which, apparently, led upward into the mouth of the third canyon. The horse was well on his way, then, to Spirit Face. Half an hour had been wasted in useless search.

Suddenly a puma rose slowly from beside one of the rocks that lined the rim of the embankment above Mak. Panting, eyes glazed from thirst, the big cat stared down at Mak less than twenty feet below.

Mak's heart raced. He became overpoweringly aware of being alone. He thought numbly, "That cat's going to jump down on me. I can't stop him . . ."

But the cat turned and vanished like a yellow shadow beyond the rim of the wall. The suffering wild thing had let him live.

Mak began the return trip. Minutes counted, now that Shungatoga had the advantage of a head start.

He reached the juncture where he had taken the wrong turn. This time he took the left fork that led into the mouth of the third canyon.

At once the grade grew steeper, the scattering of rocks larger and closer together. Mak made detours around giant boulders and climbed over their hot, hard surfaces. All the while he kept a close watch for the fast-moving horse that must be somewhere ahead of him in the upper canyon.

His feet ached with bruises. Sweat ran from his hair and wilted the feather of his cowlick. The sun's rays, striking the rock, reflected upward into his face. He was close to suffocation.

A man could collapse and die from prolonged exposure to such terrible heat — like the cow whose mummified carcass lay in a dry wash across the way.

Hundreds of horses and cattle belonging to Indians and ranchers had been lost in the brutal terrain of Makosica. After all, it was not a matter of life and death that one horse be brought back to its owner.

Yet Mak was gripped by his promise to Cloud Rise, and by an obsession to keep going. An Indian, he was a part of the meaning and message of Makosica — survival.

He looked up and found the way ahead of him entirely blocked by another pile-up of rock. It was higher than anything that had confronted him yet. Like a great dam, the avalanche of stone spread from one wall of the canyon to the other. Its towering height hid everything that lay beyond it.

Checked by the massive obstruction, Mak felt a surge of relief. No horse could climb that mountain of loose rock. Shungatoga would be trapped by it before he ever could reach Spirit Face, which certainly lay somewhere beyond.

He was unable to see the horse anywhere in the massive spill of rock. Apparently Shungatoga rested, hidden in the shade of one of the taller boulders that were scattered near its base.

Best not to waste time threading the boulders in his

35

search. Better to climb the rocks along the opposite canyon wall for a higher vantage point from which to locate the horse.

The rocks made a rough stairway to the canyon's rim. Mak began to climb it.

With the first step he stumbled and skinned his knee on a sharp edge. Sweat burned into it, but he kept climbing until finally he reached the rim of the canyon.

He stood there, panting, looking down upon the rock spill for sight of the fleeing horse. Then he saw Shungatoga immediately to his left, climbing up the rocks the way he himself had come.

Mak watched the lunging, straining horse come up the last rocks of the steep, crude stairway. Sides heaving, streaked with sweat, the horse paused beside two adjacent boulders only a few yards opposite Mak.

Impossible that any horse could have made that steep, treacherous climb. Unless . . .

It had to be the power of the Spirit Face that drew Shungatoga safely up the rocks and ever closer!

Almost at once the horse discovered Mak. He swung around as though to return to the canyon floor. Mak leaped toward him, cornering him between the two towering boulders.

Shungatoga reared, seeking a way forward across the rough rocky rim. As he swiveled, Mak swung the loop of rope toward the tossing white head. It was a good throw. Mak knew he had his horse.

Then, with the loop of rope whistling through the air, Mak's arm dropped lifelessly to his side. The coil wavered, fell unnoticed to the ground at the horse's hoofs.

Mak found himself staring across the obstruction of rock, beyond the cornered horse, and straight into Spirit Face on the opposite canyon wall only a stone's throw away.

No mistaking it. The face was set in the wall exactly as legend had it. There was the protruding rounded curve of the half-open mouth, its grin filled with rows of huge jagged teeth. On each side of the overhanging nose were two cavernous eyes. Their hideous hollows were shaded by the jutting shelf of sandstone that formed the forehead.

Mak stared through the blazing heat as if frozen. His rope trailed from his hand while his eyes remained fixed upon the hideous features on the wall beyond.

Dully he heard the thud of hoofs as the horse leaped free of the boulder trap and onto the canyon's rim. Mak watched Shungatoga plunge directly past him while he stood as if hypnotized, unable to make another throw.

He let the horse trot briskly away from him along the rim of the canyon toward a rock ledge that projected itself directly beneath the stone face across the way.

Mak tried to shout at Shungatoga to frighten him away from Spirit Face. His voice dried up in his throat.

In the quivering heat, Spirit Face seemed to shake with mocking laughter. Slyly, its power drew the white horse closer.

Shungatoga gained the ledge, and stood directly beneath Spirit Face. Caught in the power of the evil spirit above him, he tossed his white head and stamped his forefoot, challenging Mak to come closer with his rope.

Now the grinning face reached out from the wall to

blow its breath at Mak. The fiery blast made him reel. The white horse on the ledge became a swaying ghost horse before his eyes.

Mak forgot his mission, his promise to Cloud Rise. He must get away from the grip of that evil spirit or he, too, would be lost in its power.

He turned to escape into the floor of the canyon with its mountain of stone. In his haste he slipped and fell head-long over a rock embedded in the rim. Coming to his feet, he found that his right hand clutched a small loosened bit of stone. He started to throw it aside, but part of him said to keep it, and he couldn't seem to make it leave his hand.

The slender finger-length bit looked something like the bone of an animal, except that it felt like stone. A small hole ran lengthwise down the center — like one of Mary's long hollow beads.

What kind of strange thing was this? No time now to figure it out. Mechanically Mak slipped his find into a jeans pocket and plunged down the side of the canyon. He was consumed with only one thought — to put Spirit Face out of his sight as fast as he could.

Just then he heard the pound of hoofs beating the rocky ground behind him. He glanced over his shoulder. To his amazement, Shungatoga had left his ghost. He had left the ledge. His hoofs threw up dust and small pebbles as he galloped in Mak's direction. He came on swiftly, freely, as though the hold of Spirit Face suddenly was broken.

Mak could not believe what he saw. His shaking hands began to grope for the loosened rope that trailed behind him. It would take but a moment more to coil it — if the fleeing horse passed close enough — and if he threw well —

Shungatoga came on. Mak's hand lifted. The loop shot out against a final blast of heat from the face on the canyon wall. It was a bad throw, but by a fluke the wobbly noose settled about the neck of the horse as he galloped past.

Mak braced himself against a boulder to check the pull of the captured animal. Then, without looking back, he led the horse down the rocky bank to the canyon floor.

Finally the mountain of rock hid Spirit Face from sight. Mak drew Shungatoga close and swung to his back.

Half an hour later he rode bareback out of the gorge below Big Bench to the shaded boulder where Nite Boy stood waiting.

How had he ever got away from that evil spell on the canyon wall? Some power had been at work to protect him. A strong power, it had to be, to help him rope a lost horse at the very foot of one of the spirits that had destroyed the grasslands of his people.

As he transferred to his own saddle on Nite Boy, Mak's arm brushed the pocket of his jeans. He felt a small hard lump there and remembered the strange little bone of stone he had found when he fell. He clutched it through the fabric of his pants.

It came to him that the evil spell over the horse was broken the moment he had pocketed that tiny object. He had found it in danger. He had caught Shungatoga — released from his ghost — with a bad throw, then made a safe escape. More important, this small bit of stone held a deep personal meaning for him. He had been led to it through a struggle with himself to keep his word, to hold to his birthright.

Then he knew beyond a doubt. That strange bit of stone in his pocket was his wa-sic, his personal power.

He had won his spirit at last!

7 What Now, Wa-sic?

Mary laid aside a pair of moccasins she had just finished beading. From her arbor lookout she saw Mak return Cloud Rise's lost horse to him. She heard the old Indian singing in the hot wind, as he rode his Shungatoga away.

She asked no questions. She brought Mak a piece of cold meat and a cup of water.

Mak drew the stone-bone from his pocket and held it in his outstretched palm. "My wa-sic," he announced.

Mary examined the small piece, noting its strangeness.

"I found it below Spirit Face on the canyon wall," he told her simply. "It kept me safe while I roped Cloud Rise's horse there."

Mary clasped her hand over her mouth in the Indian sign of consternation and awe. She lifted her head and let him see the pride in her eyes.

There was a moment of closeness between them.

Then Mary threaded a fine leather cord through the hollow in the small strange object and hung it about Mak's neck. It was the way many of their tribesmen wore their power pieces. It was the way Mary wore her own bundle of power, filled with sacred symbols, close to her bare bosom — a tiny blue feather, a squirrel's paw, Mak's baby tooth.

"Wasta," she said softly, as though a dream had come true for her, too.

The shadow of the leaf arbor spread its midafternoon length to the rim of the coulee, and day was wasting. Mary gave no sign about what was expected of the power of his wa-sic before another sunrise.

She began to wrap the finished moccasins in a sheet of newspaper.

"I take these moccasins to Barrack Ranch," she told Mak.

"Barracks are moving to Whitehorn," he reminded her.

"I still hear their dog bark."

True, only hours ago he had seen the Barrack girl ride by with her dog. Yaller, she called him. It seemed months ago, instead of hours.

Mak watched Mary finish wrapping the moccasins. Each happening, the least word or move, must have meaning and direction for him now. Any minute might bring a sign that would lead him to his place in the land of his people — for all the packed bags Pop had set on the doorstep at Halfway House.

At sunrise tomorrow Pop would leave for California, and planned to take him along. Mary would break camp

41

and go to live in Antelope with her sister. She had to dismantle her tepee, gather her simple belongings — her blankets, a kettle and skillet, a dress or two, the box that held her great-grandfather's cherished headdress.

To give her time to load her wagon — to give himself time — Mak offered cautiously, "I could ride over to Barracks' with the moccasins."

Mary shook her head. "They are special. I will take them. I want to fix something over there before I go away."

She got to her feet with the package and motioned Mak to follow. "You come."

Fix what? A great-granddaughter of Chief Earth Boy, Mary's power was strong. Did she have a sign for him, now that he had proven himself?

Mary gave no explanation, and he dared not press it, for fear of destroying a vague, last-minute hope. Anyway, there was nothing to be gained by remaining behind, with the bags packed in readiness and Pop nodding over his afternoon nap.

Mak followed Mary down the slope of the coulee, past the gas pumps shrouded in rusty silence, past the corral. She shook off the idea of riding Nite Boy. He was tired and hungry. It was only a two-mile walk to Barracks'.

At the open, wire-snarled gate, Mary stepped aside for Mak to pass through first, after the way of an Indian woman in company with a man.

A new pride lifted Mak's heart, yet for a moment he felt oddly let down and helpless. By her simple gesture Mary Sits told him that his spirit power had cut forever the boyhood ties that bound him to her. He was in the making of a man.

He led the way across the borders of the reservation in the direction of Barrack Ranch on the western rim of the badlands. A giant cottonwood tree towered over the distant ranchhouse, pointing the way like a sentinel through the heat waves.

They skirted the corner of the school section, marked by an iron stake driven in the center of four faint, sodded-over depressions. Pop had said that the stake and holes marked Montana State land set aside for a school, some day, for Indian and ranch children.

"Too late for me," Mak thought.

Barrack's waterhole, sucked dry by the merciless sun, was a network of open cracks. Beyond it, the rancher's field felt hot and hard under their feet, like the sidewalks in Whitehorn. With no rain to sprout it, winds had blown the seed wheat out of the ground. The powder-dry topsoil went with the seed, so that only bare hardpan remained.

Finally they came to the wide wooden ranch gate, its high posts arched with a weathered board containing the Barrack name and brand. Mak swung it open. The ranch-house stood before them, high and weathered and grimly white-man.

Mak recalled Pop saying that the first Barrack came to Montana in a covered wagon. He planted his feet and his home and his tree and his cattle on Indian land.

"My family's land," Mary had added above her bead-work.

Mak took in the well-cared-for sheds and barns, the old log bunkhouse and cooling cave, the corrals and diminished haystacks that flanked the house under the cotton-wood. At times, when riding by, he had caught glimpses of

43

tiny Mrs. Barrack feeding her white hens in the dooryard. Sometimes he saw young Jim Barrack breaking a colt at the snubbing post in the corral, too intent on his work to signal hello to an Indian passer-by. The hum of radio music from under the cottonwood and the rattle of a tractor in the fields had followed Mak long after the Barrack place was out of sight.

These white folks, what were they like? How did they talk and plan and work and live together?

Strangely, he could find little bitterness or envy in his heart toward this white family who lived on land taken from his people. Was that because he, too, had white blood in his veins? Was he traitor to his mother's people because he felt no triumph that drought was about to drive the white family from land that rightfully belonged to him and his race?

Or was it because he knew how it hurt to leave his own home that he felt no animosity toward the Barrack family?

Yaller, the cattledog, rose barking from an island of shade made by the cottonwood beside the house. Halted momentarily by the dog, Mak caught the flash of a red jeep parked beside the chokecherry trees at the corner of the old log bunkhouse. It didn't have a Barrack look.

Mary nudged him to move on. The dog, petulant in the heat, followed them to his master's door. His panting made a sound like a small engine at their heels as he sniffed the Indian scent of them.

The tree-shaded back steps offered welcome relief from the sun. Mary's dark hand reached out and pounded on the warped screen door. Mak drew back, muscles tensed. Mountain Boy had said that young Jim Barrack sent him away once when he came to borrow an ax.

Mak stood ready to bolt into the heat, should Mary and he be ordered off the premises. His hand groped across his chest to check if his wa-sic was there.

It was there.

8 Mary's Plan

The wheat rancher himself came to answer Mary's knock.

Mak knew the broad-shouldered George Barrack only from a distance — glued to his dust-clouded tractor, or bounding along the ranch road in his farm truck. Close up, his set of shoulder and weathered jaw gave the rancher the no-nonsense look of western sheriffs in school movies.

He glanced at the Indian visitors on his doorstep without speaking, almost without seeing them. Instead, as if through force of habit, his glance swept back and forth across the brassy sky above their heads.

"Looking for rain clouds," thought Mak.

Mary let the frowning rancher know at once that they were not hungry Indians come to beg a handout.

Her smile disclosed even, white teeth. "How, Mr. Bar-

rack. I am Mary Sits and he is Makosica Mike Malloy."
She jerked her thumb toward Mak. Aware of the rancher's
acquaintance with Pop Williams, she added, "We come
from Halfway House. I made some moccasins for your
girl. You call her, please?"

Mary tore the newspaper wrapping from her package,
revealing a pair of slim buckskin moccasins with an elabo-
rate flower design banding arch and toe.

Mr. Barrack scarcely glanced at the careful native
handiwork. "My daughter has bought all the moccasins
she needs for her beadwork collection," he said, and
moved to close the screen door.

Mak thought how drought and the pain of leaving his
land might close the rancher's mind to fancy stitching. Not
so Mary. She slipped her moccasined foot inside the door
to hold it open.

Mak caught his breath. What was Mary up to?

The great-granddaughter of a warrior chieftain explained her mission in quiet dignity with her toe in the
white man's door.

"These moccasins are not for her to pay with money. I
made them free, for your girl's birthday surprise. All the
time she buys beadwork, helps us out. She is our *coza* —
our friend. Tomorrow I go away. Today I pay her back."

A faint smile erased the rancher's shortness. "Gail will
be surprised and glad that you know her birthday."

"Yes. You call her then, please?"

Hearing their voices, Gail Barrack came to push the
door wide and stand beside her father.

Today she was barefooted and in shorts instead of riding jeans, with her long yellow hair hanging in braids

46

down her back. She recognized Mak at once.

"Hi, Mak," she smiled.

"Hi." Mak grinned, relaxing a little.

Mary Sits thrust the moccasins toward Gail Barrack like treasure on a deerskin shield. "For your birthday today," she said, beaming.

Delighted, the ranch girl began naming off the softly-colored beads. "Blue, yellow, pastel pink — just like the colors in the badlands! The sky, the rocks, the peaks."

"Yes, same color as Makosica," Mary agreed modestly.

Gail stooped to slip the moccasins on her bare feet. Her blond braids fell forward. In moccasins and braids, with her deep tan and brown eyes, Mak thought Gail Barrack might pass for a mix-blooded Indian girl.

Her brother, Jim Barrack, had the same thought as he joined his sister and father in the open doorway.

"Sacagawea Yellow Hair," he teased.

He nodded at Mak, known to him as one of many Indian riders who reined off the road to let his pickup race by. Lifting muscular arms, he stretched and yawned as though interrupted from a nap. Mak appraised the young rancher's stocky build, his tobacco-brown hair, and strong blunt hands. He's only a little older, Mak thought, but in a scuffle he could take me down with one swing.

Gail extended her moccasined foot to admire it. She poked her brother's bare torso with her elbow. "Move back, lug, so Mom can see, too."

"Gorgeous!" Tiny Mrs. Barrack edged between son and daughter to approve the birthday moccasins. She, too, wore shirt and shorts. Mak thought she looked like Gail's older sister except for her graying hair, looped plainly over

47

her ears and knotted in a neat high bun.

She smiled at Mak when Gail introduced them, then turned to Mary. "But how in the world did you know Gail's birth date — or her shoe size?"

"My Dream came and told me," Mary replied simply. "And I throw Mak in for good measure, too," she added, smug in her generosity.

Having won family attention, Mary turned to George Barrack as head of the house to drive a well-planned bargain. "Pop's off to California to retire. So Halfway House gets torn down. Mak will not go. Not good for him to be alone in Makosica. So you can keep Mak here. He will make a good choreboy around your place. He can shoot rabbits for your stew. He can bring you all kinds of good luck so you will not have to leave your land for Whitehorn. He has strong wa-sic, that boy."

Mary ran her forefinger around the cord on Mak's neck and lifted the little bone of stone to display proof of his usefulness and power.

Mak drew back. What was Mary saying about him before these people? Tossing him in like a stray calf on a deal with a girl's birthday gift. Playing on the white man's sympathy for an orphaned Indian boy.

Yet — keep him as their choreboy. Bring them good luck. Make their home his home . . .

The four Barracks considered him from their doorstep. Mak waited for their answer.

Jim Barrack was first to speak. "Hey, fella, let's have a look at that!"

His hand shot out. He caught the leather cord that held Mak's wa-sic and pulled him up another step for a closer look. His smoke-blue eyes were inches from Mak's face while he turned the sacred Indian token over in his fingers.

"Looks like part of a fossilized bone or tooth of some prehistoric animal." An undercurrent of excitement threaded Jim's words.

Mak was angered by the young rancher's grip and the way the leather cord cut into his neck. "I call it wa-sic," he said.

"It's his power," Mary informed Jim Barrack.

The rancher's son gave a short laugh. "Power, wa-sic, fossil, whatever — it just could be a break for the Barrack family. Did you find it in the badlands, Mak?"

Mak hesitated. "Sure."

Holding to the wa-sic, Jim turned to Gail and his parents behind him in the doorway. "Good thing Chuck Engle hasn't left for his college." He grinned. "All Chuck needs is a fossil like this to keep him here on a real fossil hunt."

Jim Barrack's grasshopper thoughts leaped, as though massing together parts of some incomplete plan. "We might have a ready-made guide for Chuck, too." His direct eyes searched Mak's face. "How well do you know the badlands, Mak?"

Guide? Hunt? What was this pushy rancher's son getting him into? Jim Barrack held to the wa-sic as if it were his, gave it his own strange name, linked it to a strange kind of hunt. Les Bentarm had said a "college guy" at Barrack Ranch was hunting "souvenirs." That explained Chuck Engle and the red jeep. Les warned against showing whites over Indian land, too. Taking anything off of it.

Mary said from the bottom step, "Mak, he knows Mak-

49

osica like his opened hand. He lives here all his life."

Why didn't Mary keep out of this? Her interference only spurred Jim Barrack on.

"Can you guide us to the place in the badlands where you found this fossil?"

Mak stiffened. Return to that dreaded spot below Spirit Face? The very thought of return was like giant hands twisting him apart.

He answered shortly. "I know where I found my wa-sic all right, but — "

"If you know where you found it," Jim interrupted, "then that's all there is to it. You've put yourself in line for a job as Chuck Engle's guide, as well as the job of our ranch choreboy."

"But I didn't say." Anger, sparked by fear, dimmed Mak's new hope.

"This is your chance, Mak. Any other young Indian around here would jump at it. You can't lose, man."

Jim released his hold on the leather cord and looped his muscular arm about Mak's shoulders. He inserted right thumb and forefinger into his mouth and blew a shrill whistle across the dooryard in the direction of the bunk-house. "Hey, Chuck! Come out of the sack and get over here. I've found a whale of a fossil for you."

"Leave Chuck alone," Gail scolded Jim. "He's bushed from hunting fossils all week. He needs rest for an early start back to his college tomorrow morning."

"Chuck's not going back to his college tomorrow, Sis." Jim turned to his father. "Looks like we've got a chance to keep the ranch after all. What do you say, Dad?"

"I say you're taking an awful lot for granted on one

50

small bit of fossil," his father answered dryly. "Your college friend has searched the badlands all week and found nothing at all. You know because you helped him."

A dust-devil whirled the loose skin of George Barrack's wheat field toward the sky and faded it into nothingness. The rancher's eyes followed it. He was closed to all hope of saving his rangeland by any means except through the natural gift of rain.

It was not so with his son. There had to be another way, and Jim was out to find it.

"But here's a promising fossil, Dad. And an Indian guide. That makes Chuck's search worth another try. Look, Dad." Jim argued with his eye on the bunkhouse door and his hold on Mak. "Geologists passing through the badlands have seen signs of fossil remains here for years. Chuck Engle's a geologist, a top paleontologist. Last semester, when he got leave from the college Foundation to dig for fossils, I talked him into searching our badlands this summer. If he uncovers fossil beds here, his Foundation will send out a digging expedition. His men will be quartered at our place. Their board money will keep us going. We won't have to leave. Yet."

"We've been over all that before," his father said. "It's that 'if' I can't take for granted — even with the help of an Indian guide and his fossil power."

Mr. Barrack smiled into Mak's confused face — a warm, apologetic, almost fatherly smile.

Gail sided with her brother. "With Mak's help, it's worth another try, Dad. Even if Chuck fails again, we can't be any worse off than we are now. If he and Mak succeed, well" — Mak caught her quick-drawn breath — "then we can stay on at the ranch. Besides," she added brightly, "a fossil find will give Chuck a chance to earn his professorship."

Her father smiled. "Two feathers in two separate caps."

"You think this fossil hunt is some hare-brained project I dreamed up at college last year, don't you?" Jim accused his father.

"But it's a lot more sensible than Jim's other idea of crossing zebras with domestic mares," Gail added.

"This fossil project is going to work because it *is* sensible," Jim affirmed. "It's got to work. I plan to accomplish things at this ranch, and a worthwhile fossil find could make it possible."

Mr. Barrack shook his head. "I'd hate to have you lose, son."

Mak Malloy stared from father to son while they argued. He thought how he had argued with his father — about remaining in Makosica.

Jim went on, with strong feeling in his words. "For over a hundred years we Barracks have fought blizzards and grasshoppers and drought and God knows what else in order to hold to this land. Great-grandpa Barrack made good here with cattle. You and your father did all right with wheat. Until drought came. I plan to raise horses. I have a right to my chance, too. I'm not about to be the Barrack that loses his chance and his land without a fight. Whether it rains or not."

A blanket of silence spread over the group around the ranch door. The eyes of father and son held for a moment, bound by respect for one another and love for the land.

A telephone bell sounded faintly from somewhere indoors. It reminded Mak of bells jingling on ankles of warriors in the war dance.

Mr. Barrack turned to answer the ring. Mak had a feeling that the big-shouldered rancher was relieved to get away, to let the younger generation of Barracks work out the problem — if they could.

Mrs. Barrack slipped after her husband to attend to a kettle on the kitchen stove.

As though to fill the family gap, Gail Barrack sidled across the step in her birthday moccasins to stand beside Jim and Mak. With Jim's arm still looped across his shoulders, Mak felt himself held as part of a tight young threesome. He knew that Jim Barrack was not known for friendly holds on Indians, yet . . .

What was happening to him on the white rancher's doorstep?

Strange words, strange feelings, strange fears, rained about his head like arrows, all missing their mark. Fossil . . . paleontologist . . . expedition . . . guide . . . with Spirit Face coming again to rear its wicked head over them all.

They took it for granted that he was a part of their fight to hold to their home.

Didn't they know he was different from them? Their frightening plans could lead him into trouble. Why didn't Mary do something, squatting now in the shade of the cottonwood, chewing her coffee bean? He should wrench free of Jim Barrack's arm, get away on his Indian-runner legs.

Yet a need of his own rooted him there.

Jim Barrack said, "Here comes Chuck. Now we'll get this thing wrapped up!"

9 About Those Fossil Things

Mak watched the slight, bearded "college guy" whip around his red jeep beside the bunkhouse door. He crossed the dooryard in long strides, then halted at the ranchhouse steps.

Jim Barrack made a hasty apology from the doorway. "Sorry to cut off your sleep, Chuck, but my good news can't wait. I've found you a first-rate fossil, along with a first-rate guide. Mak Malloy here."

"And Mary Sits." Gail was quick to include her Indian friend, still seated in the shade of the cottonwood.

"Great!" Chuck Engle's enthusiastic smile welcomed his meeting with the two Indians. In the same breath he welcomed Jim's good news.

"Actually, Chuck is Dr. Charles Engle," Gail explained to Mary and Mak. "Not a medical doctor, but a paleontologist with a college degree. Paleontologist, in simple words, means bone man. Chuck makes it his life's work to find rocks and old bones in the earth's crust — besides teaching about them. Jim met him at college last year and brought him back to fossil-hunt. He's all right, and we hope to keep him here a long time." Gail flashed an admiring smile at her brother's college friend.

Dr. Charles Engle, paleontologist, showed the ranch girl a brisk salute.

54

Mak reminded himself that teachers, for all their smiles and good manners, could get you to do things you didn't like. Yet, this Engle fellow seemed hardly Mak's idea of a teacher, in his bulging glasses and grubby beard and wrinkled jeans. A week of hunting fossils under the harsh Montana sun and wind had turned his thin pink skin to a peeling red. He had thwarted the sunburn on his nose with a thick triangular coating of white ointment. Mak thought it looked a little like war paint.

"And Mak's real name, Chuck, is Makosica Mike Malloy," Gail said, rounding out the introductions. "He and Mary come from Pop Williams' Halfway House in the reservation badlands, two miles to the east of us."

Charles Engle noted Mak's fair skin, his stiff brown hair, and flecked hazel eyes with no show of surprise. "So you are named for the badlands," he said, smiling at Mak. *"Mako* for land. *Sica* for bad. Right?"

"Right." Mak nodded, startled that the man from the distant college should know even two words of the language of his people. "It's the desertland in our country," he added.

"Let's get off names and on with the fossil," Jim Barrack interrupted. "Take a look at it, Chuck." Jim indicated the small ivorylike stone hanging crosswise on its leather cord over Mak's bare chest.

"It's called wa-sic," Mak said, determined to be correct about that name, also.

His heartbeat quickened as the nearsighted Engle stepped close to examine the wa-sic through his thick lenses.

"Isn't Indian wa-sic a kind of charm or good luck

55

piece?" he asked Mak, turning the small fossil idly in his slender fingers. "I mean, something like the rabbit's foot that we white folks carry about?"

Mak doubted the comparison. No use to explain that Indian wa-sic was the sacred symbol of self and spirit, rooted in the land, which was the measure of all life. No white man could understand. Not even Pop, who had called wa-sic "superstitious nonsense."

"It's my power," Mak told Engle and let it go at that.

"This small fossil might hold considerable power, all right," Dr. Engle agreed. "It may be part of the buried skeleton of a mastodon — a powerful prehistoric beast that roamed the Montana badlands millions of years ago, before the Age of Man."

"I don't know the name of the animal or when it came," Mak said shortly. "Our medicine men haven't told us about such animals."

Engle left the fossil on Mak's chest along with the subject of prehistoric animals. "I understand that a young Indian's power usually is found while meeting with great danger."

Mak dropped a mask of wariness over his face. What was this young bone man from the college trying to sniff out with his white-painted nose? And with his talk about strange animals on Indian land that no Indian ever heard about? His soft words sounded like a follow-up to Jim Barrack's earlier questions, which led to dangerous ground.

"I roped a horse there," he told Engle. "In danger."

Jim Barrack broke in. "What do you mean, danger?"

"I mean the place where I found it is a dangerous place."

"You mean it's only dangerous for Indians to go to?"

Jim Barrack's smoky eyes probed Mak's closed face. He knew little about his Indian neighbors, cared less about their beliefs, but right now he needed Indian help. He did not intend to be blocked by a wall of primitive belief.

Mak stiffened, sensing the drift of Jim's suspicion.

Dr. Charles Engle caught the rise of hostility between his rancher friend and Indian neighbor. Success of a renewed fossil hunt was important to him, too. He broke in agreeably. "I can well believe that there are dozens of dangerous spots in Makosica, Mak. I doubt if any man fully realizes the dangers in your great and terrible land. Not any white man, I mean."

Engle glanced eastward, toward Makosica, where the shadowy forms of spires and benches crouched beneath the haze of heat. "Frankly, one week of searching its mere perimeter for fossils has scared me out," he admitted honestly. "I never can succeed without the help of a good guide. Even Jim, who has lived next door to it all his life, had to give up."

Jim's good-natured shrug acknowledged truth in Engle's words. "I'm a horseman, not an explorer. With Mak, it's different. Mak knows the badlands like the palm of his hand," Jim told Engle, parroting Mary's words. "And he'll be here at our ranch ready for guide work. We've offered him the job of choreboy for his room and board."

Now was the time to speak up, say no to this crazy kind of talk.

Mrs. Barrack stepped to the door from her kitchen. Her voice was alive with warmth and friendliness. "And we have plenty of room for you, too, Mak," she said. "I'll make up the extra bunk in the bunkhouse for you, along with Chuck."

Mr. Barrack, at his wife's shoulder, announced, "The manager of the Whitehorn Garage just phoned. He's ready for me to begin work next Monday." The smile he gave Mak through the screen door ironed out the frown lines between his eyes. "We'll be needing an extra hand at the ranch, Mak, to help look after things while I'm away during the week."

Mak managed a stiff grin. He should tell this kindly white rancher and his wife no. Why did the word stick in his throat?

Beside him Gail threw back her braids at the promising turn of events. "With Mak around to help look after things, Jim, you'll be free to ride off on your wild horse hunt for as long as you like. You really can go out for that rodeo award money. Could we ever use *that!*"

Mak stared at Gail Barrack, then at her brother. Wild horse hunt? The only wild horses around were those in the herd led by the appaloosa stallion on Big Bench. The horse he himself planned to capture some day. Backed by his wa-sic, Jim Barrack and he together should be able to —

His whirlwind dream began to clear a path through a maze of fears and needs. If he took them up on their offer, he could do a lot for himself. He could help the ranch family, and the smart college guy —

They waited, unable to believe that he could find reason to slight their generosity — the anxious girl, her determined brother, their parents, the pink-faced bone man. And Mary sucking her coffee bean, waiting for him to fight out his problem.

Yet he remained under his blanket of silence and his fear.

From somewhere under the steps Yaller snuffled his way loudly after a flea.

A casual suggestion from Charles Engle broke the silence. "Why not take the job of guide on trial for a few days, Mak? While you are making up your mind whether or not to stay on, we can do some preliminary explorations without concentrating on any particular fossil spot. We'll scout around for fossils wherever you choose to guide me. Who knows," he smiled, "we might find enough fossils in a general badlands survey to keep us busy all summer."

Was this mild-speaking bone man taking him off the hook by making the guide job appear easy and safe and temporary, until by some roundabout way, Mak would be led into serious trouble?

Charles Engle's quiet voice went on, reassuring him. "Certainly you can lead me to many points of interest in your Makosica that might reveal fossils. Unusual land formations, caves, mineral deposits, Indian pictographs perhaps."

Pictographs. Vaguely, Mak linked the unfamiliar word with the Indian picture writings on the walls of the cave in the coulee below Halfway House.

Then there were those half-forgotten holes on Rattlesnake Ridge. Round and shallow, set evenly apart, like postholes in dried mud. Only who would dig postholes out there? He never returned to Rattlesnake Ridge following his uneasy discovery.

Sure, he could stay with the Barracks and guide Charles Engle to dozens of strange rocks and markings. Far from the spot where he found his wa-sic. In a few days' time.

Dr. Engle's questioning, sunburned face shone with sweat. He had a feeling for Indian people, their names, their language, their beliefs, their land. He did not pry or demand or take too much for granted. He did not try to change the name of a sacred Indian power piece. Like Pop, Dr. Engle left Mak to choose for himself. As Gail said, he was "all right."

A faint smile broke across Mak's sober face. "Okay, then," he heard himself saying to Dr. Charles Engle, "but before we go to look, maybe you should tell me more about those fossil things."

Jim broke out with a glad yelp. Gail jumped to her feet. "Chuck will tell you all about fossils at dinner, Mak. I've heard a lot of table talk about them, but I want to know more. What a birthday party *I* am going to have!"

She reached Mak's hand and pulled him into the kitchen. "Come, take a look at my birthday cake."

Mrs. Barrack was placing a cake studded with pink candles on a long table draped in white, like the altar in the school chapel on the river. She smiled at him, and the homey scent of her kitchen closed about him.

Mak pawed self-consciously at his hair to smooth it. He reached a second time toward his crown to tame the bristly cowlick.

Gail laughed. "Forget it, Mak. It belongs that way. Here." She offered him a match. "Help me light these candles. There're sixteen of them this year, too many for me to light alone."

As Mak turned to take the match he caught a movement out of the open doorway. It was Mary, passing through the ranch gate on her way to live with her sister. On her way out of his life.

He had gathered all his strength from Mary. Now she left him in a strange home with white people, and with a strange new job he hadn't totally promised to fulfill.

He struck the match clumsily and it broke. His wa-sic swung awry on his chest. He jerked it straight. Held to it.

After all, what did he have to be afraid of?

The power of his wa-sic, together with Mary's plan, had got him a home in the badlands country.

He took a second match. And the first tiny flame stood out like a native ceremonial torch on the white girl's birthday cake.

10 Choreboy

On Monday morning, along with the rest of the family, Mak waved Mr. Barrack off to begin his first week of work at the Whitehorn Garage.

Charles Engle was compelled to follow him two days later with his broken-down jeep in tow. The long trip west and his unsuccessful forays into the rugged badlands country had developed a knock in the sturdy engine.

Jim and Engle had tried to make repairs at the ranch.

"We'll have to call the Reeser boys from over the ridge to tow it to Whitehorn," Jim said finally. "The garage may have to send for parts. Even with Dad there to work on it, it may take the rest of this week to get it running."

Engle turned apologetically to Mak, his pink face blotched with car grease. "Which means we'll need to postpone our fossil hunt until the next week."

"That's okay." Mak turned to gather up the wrenches and return them to the tool shed. He felt relieved at the delay.

"I don't call it okay," Jim said. "I call it bad luck."

Gail could find good in every misfortune. "Anyway, you'll have a few extra days, Mak, to get onto the lay of the ranch. And Chuck, you will be staying with Dad at Aunt Martha's house in Whitehorn. You can get acquainted with that side of our family while the jeep's being repaired."

"Aunt Martha is matriarch of the Barrack cattle barons," Jim explained to Engle. "Maybe she can hurry up the garage mechanics. She's been known to twist many a tail to get things moving."

Charles Engle went along with Gail, good-naturedly making the best of his interrupted fossil project. "I may have a chance to get acquainted with some of the reservation Indians, too, while waiting around Whitehorn. I'll need a permit from their Tribal Council before excavating fossils on Indian land."

Mak dropped a hammer, retrieved it.

A request by Charles Engle to dig for fossils — to scarify their Mother, the Earth — was sure to stir up tribal suspicion and resentment. His people would remember other land deals with white men where the Indians got the worst of it. Wars had been fought over that.

Mak answered Engle over his shoulder on his way to the tool shed. "The Indians trade in Whitehorn. You'll see some of them there, sir."

Jim Barrack caught a tightness in the young Indian's voice. He refused to give it a second thought.

Now it was nearing the close of Mak's first week as chore-boy at Barrack Ranch. Tomorrow Mr. Barrack expected to return from Whitehorn for the weekend, along with Engle, his red jeep in good shape to start the fossil hunt on Monday.

Mak turned the milch cow out of the stanchion, then took up a pail to draw water for the chickens from the stock well in the coulee. Yaller whisked ahead of him, showing the way.

63

"The water level is sinking fastest in the well close to the house," Jim had explained. "So we'll have to be saving on that water. Trouble is, we can't use the stock well for the house because drainage from the barns and corral makes it unsanitary for human use."

Mak knew nothing about water levels or drainage or sanitation. But he got the message. If it didn't rain soon, the house well would go dry. The family would be without safe drinking water.

It was early morning, yet sweat beaded Mak's forehead when he climbed the steep banks of the coulee with the brimming pail. He stopped to get his breath. Yaller jumped on him, inviting play.

Mak caught up a stick and threw it across the corral for the cattledog to retrieve. Intent on the arc of the stick, Yaller nearly collided with Gail's paint pony, dozing in the shade of the log cattle shed. Touchy with heat, Paint laid back his ears at Yaller, already bounding away with his trophy.

Mak laughed. "All right for you, Paint."

All right for everything — for the games of checkers Gail let him win in the shade of the cottonwood; for short sprints with Jim between corral and house at mealtime, which his Indian-runner legs did not always let Jim win; for the hunger that twisted his stomach as Mrs. Barrack pulled pungent cinnamon rolls out of the oven while singing her song about some saints gathering at the river — "the beautiful, the beautiful river."

A white woman's prayer song it was, asking for cold, beautiful water to flood her dying grasslands, fill her wells and dried-out waterholes. Fill her life with hope.

Mak poured water into the chickens' drinking pan. Then he turned toward the woodpile to chop kindling for the evening meal before the heat of midday. As he passed the bunkhouse, he paused to peer into the open doorway.

Occupied by Barrack cowboys in the early cattle-ranching days, the low log building had stood unused for years, except as a catchall for grain sacks, garden gear, and discarded saddles. Scrubbed and curtained now for Engle and himself, the single room looked cool and inviting with its log walls hugging the earth, its sides shaded by choke-cherry bushes.

A homemade rawhide chair stood at the reading table beside Engle's bunk. Mak resisted the temptation to step inside to rest and cool off.

A short neat row of Engle's books lined the shelf above his bunk. They were the first objects to meet Mak's eyes when he wakened in the morning. He had helped Engle unload them from the jeep when his own arrival at the ranch encouraged Engle to remain.

"Here is a picture of a dinosaur from the Age of Reptiles." Engle had pointed to a photo of an animal skeleton. "Eighty feet long, weighed several tons, but had only one pound of brains, I understand. And a skeleton of a small, three-toed horse that died in a lake basin a million years ago. The triceratops pictured here," Dr. Engle went on, flipping the pages, "has been excavated in Wyoming, Montana, and Colorado. Looks something like a bull-dozer, doesn't he?"

"Sort of." Mak grinned, remembering the bulldozers that had helped to build the reservation highway with their giant clanks and rumbles.

"Nothing mysterious about fossils, Mak," Engle had assured him at Gail Barrack's birthday dinner. "Fossils are a real and ordinary part of nature. Just old bones that earth pressures and minerals and time have turned to stone."

Too much that was not real or ordinary came at Mak that first evening at the Barracks'. The orderly table and shining old silver with heads bowed in prayer over it; the different delicious foods. And the strange talk describing a group of great animals called mastodons that were said to have left their bones in his homeland.

"Movements of the earth's crust," Dr. Engle went on, "and erosion by wind and rain — sometimes by highway bulldozers — brought them to the surface."

"Where you just happened to stumble over the chip of fossil you call your wa-sic," Jim put in. "Okay?" Jim had closed the discussion by reaching for another piece of birthday cake.

Okay, that his sacred wa-sic was an ordinary thing? And that it belonged to some strange ancient Makosica animal never once mentioned in Indian legend?

Okay, that he "just happened" to find it for his power in that terrifying ordeal before Spirit Face?

He did not need to believe all this talk. White people said many things that Indians could not believe. He would guide Dr. Engle for mastodon fossils — for a few days. He would not worry about how they came to be there. So he thought that first evening.

"You'll not really understand about fossils, Mak, until you dig for them, study about them, assemble them," Dr. Engle said afterward in the bunkhouse. He scattered an array of rocks and small fossilized bones among his books and along the windowsills. "Makes the room more homey," he said and grinned at Mak.

He set up name cards to identify an agatized fossil tooth found in a foreign land, a baby elephant's toe embedded in sedimentary rock. "You've probably come across fossils like these dozens of times, Mak," he said. "You just haven't recognized them as such."

Mak doubted that. Yet there were those odd-looking rocks with shell-like imprints he'd gathered from rock spills and caves all over Makosica. Tourists had paid good prices for these mysterious mementos of the Montana badlands.

"But what comes of all this?" he asked cautiously of Charles Engle. "What good are old bones from dead animals that have turned to stone?"

He could ask the troublesome question then, when he and the bone man were alone in the bunkhouse.

"Fossilized bones of excavated prehistoric animals are fastened together carefully into skeletons of the entire animal — like the pictures in my books. Then the skeletons are set up in museums for thousands of people to see."

"But why *see?*"

"When men study these fossilized skeletons, Mak, they learn from them. Their bones tell scientists such as myself what the earth was like in prehistoric time, that is, centuries before the Age of Man. From such ancient facts we learn about ourselves, how we got here, how we have grown to become what we are today. We learn to understand ourselves and one another. But here I go lecturing."

Dr. Engle smiled apologetically into Mak's confused eyes. "Let's talk about something close at hand."

He lifted a scuffed leather case from a packing box and removed a pair of binoculars. "These powerful glasses are handy for locating fossils. Take a look," he invited, pleased as a boy showing off his toys to a new friend.

Mak held the heavy glasses to his eyes. Dr. Engle turned him to face the open bunkhouse door, adjusted a screw. The sun had set, but the long western twilight was bright as day.

Suddenly an animal jumped out at Mak through the powerful lenses. It was a jackrabbit, leaping across the sage beyond the ranch gate. The binoculars brought it inches before him — like one of those eighty-foot animals with little brains in Dr. Engle's books.

Startled, Mak returned the glasses.

"What did you see, Mak?" Dr. Engle inquired.

"I saw — far."

How far could the strange power in those glasses reach?

Could it reach across Makosica to the face on the canyon wall?

Pop Williams had asked questions that first week, too.

"I don't savvy all this fossil business that George Barrack talks about," Pop said.

He had stopped by the ranch to bid Mak goodbye on his way to California, having given grudging consent to George Barrack to keep Mak at Barrack Ranch. He had brought Mak's warbag and radio in his pickup with Nite Boy trotting behind.

"What's the good of this fossil stuff after you and this college chap find it, anyway?" A doubtful testiness tinged

Pop's scratchy old voice. He was out of sorts because Mary had interfered with his plan to take Mak to California.

Numbly Mak shook his head. He was too mixed up to understand it himself. How could he explain?

Pop pulled out a red handkerchief to mop his sweaty face. He daubed at a watery eye. "If this fossil thing doesn't pan out," he warned Mak finally, "I'll send you a ticket to follow me to California. Understand?"

Mak swallowed. "I understand."

Pop's scratchy voice made it clear that he had a way out if things got rough. Mak's heart felt like a stone in his chest.

Pop wiped his teary eye again. "Well," he said. They shook hands awkwardly.

Mak stood in the dooryard, fingering his wa-sic. And staring after the testy old-timer who had raised him like a white boy. Soon, all he could see of Pop was a feather of dust lifting above the horizon.

Halfway House, the truckers and tourists, seemed to fade into the dust along with Pop.

He was all caught up in a new way of life.

Somehow this "fossil thing" must "pan out."

11 Thought I Caught It Showing

Mrs. Barrack came from the kitchen to set a bowl of potato chips and a pitcher of iced punch on the rough board table under the cottonwood.

Mak looked up at her over the freshly split kindling he was laying on the outdoor grill in readiness for the evening meal. "Something like an Indian campfire." He grinned.

She smiled under the neat bun of her hair. "Like a rancher's picnic, too. And it saves electricity."

She extended the bowl of chips. "You must be starved, Mak. It's not yet midmorning and you've done a day's work."

Her praise pleased Mak. He passed the bowl to Gail before helping himself, as he had seen Jim do for his mother.

Gail lolled in the faded canvas swing, reading a book. One moccasined foot pushed the swing idly to and fro.

She scooped up a handful of chips without lifting her eyes. "Thanks, Mak. You make me feel waited on — like Cleopatra in my story."

Mak wondered if this Cleopatra had long straight blond hair. He poured himself a drink and found a seat on a bleached cottonwood stump at the far edge of the shade.

Jim strode up in riding boots and straw hat.

"What we save on electricity," he said, having overheard his mother's remark to Mak, "our choreboy eats up in potato chips."

Mak grinned uncertainly. He wasn't always sure how to take Jim. "I mended the hole your mare kicked in the corral gate," he said. "Want me to saddle her up for you now?"

"You don't leave anything for me to do around here any more, Mak," Jim complained, pouring himself a drink.

"Except to track down that wild appaloosa mustang on Big Bench," Gail reminded her brother from over the top of her book. "And win the rodeo award. Before someone else wins it."

Jim bridled. "Anyone around here say I'm not trying?"

She knew he had ridden out day after day, that he was ready to ride again. She smiled and said, as though already he had won the award, "That prize money sure will fit okay into our skimpy budget."

"What if I choose to keep the mustang for breeding purposes," Jim countered, "rather than collect the award money for him?"

"Just so you win something," she answered lightly. "I'm not surprised at anything you do when it comes to horses."

Jim took off his hat to run blunt fingers through his tobacco-brown hair. He knew they needed money for bread and butter. "Guess I'd be lucky to win either way. That wild appaloosa over on Big Bench is as unpredictable as the badland mirages. He's there one minute, then he isn't."

Jim strode off toward the corral to get his horse, his teeth crunching potato chips, heels crunching gravel.

71

Mak remembered a more congenial talk he'd had with Jim earlier that week.

Jim had been currying his appaloosa mare in the corral that particular morning. Nite Boy and Gail's Paint stood at the water tank below them. They stamped and twitched hides impatiently at horseflies that interrupted their naps.

Mak took up a brush to help Jim with the grooming. It was one of several overtures he had made that first week to relieve the stiffness of their first meeting over the secret spot where he found his wa-sic.

He edged in a friendly comment as he brushed out Loosa's sparse mane. "George Stands-on-Iron raises appaloosas over on the reservation."

"None of them are as good as my mare," Jim said, defying Mak to doubt him.

"Right," Mak conceded cheerfully. "Your mare has everything that belongs to an appaloosa — frosted rump, leopard's spots, feet like a mule's. Except she has a pretty way of picking them up," he added lest Jim take offense at the comparison. "She has eyes like people, too, with the whites showing."

Jim grinned, surprised that Mak had given such attention to Loosa while he fed and watered her.

Mak pulled a bur from the fringe of hairs that lined the mare's ear. "Them hairs look like feathers in a play war bonnet," he grinned.

Jim said, "You know your horses, don't you, Mak, even if you don't know your grammar. It's *those* hairs, not *them* hairs."

"Indians had to know about horses — those horses got us places," Mak said correctly.

"Right. Horses got the plains Indians all over the West."

Jim Barrack knew his early American history better than he knew his early American neighbors.

He ran the currycomb across Loosa's spotted rump. "I took over the horses on this ranch as soon as I could climb into a saddle," he confided unexpectedly. "When the drought hit, Dad and I agreed it was best to keep two or three irons in the fire. His — wheat; mine — horses. That's why I went to college last year — to pick up the finer points of horse breeding. Soon as this drought's over, I plan to start breeding horses in earnest. Appaloosas, naturally. They're nearly a lost breed. Know that, Mak?"

"Don't see many around," Mak admitted, squatting to brush Loosa's foreleg. "The Nez Perce Indians over in Idaho got the appaloosas going."

"Right. And they did a good job of it, too. Appaloosas bred from that early strain are the most popular of all saddle horses today. Easy to handle, long-winded, exotic in appearance. Like Loosa here. They'll bring good prices.

The mare dipped her nose to nip at Jim's belt. "Trouble is," he added stroking the good bone of her face, "I'm going to need some top breeding stock. Stallions cost money. Unless — "

He glanced across the mare's head toward the dim outline of Big Bench where the wild appaloosa mustang lived.

He caught Mak's eye on him and shrugged. "We'll work out a breeding program — one way or another."

"Sure." *We,* Jim had said. Mak began to feel closer to him.

So now Jim was trotting his appaloosa mare briskly toward the front gate, heading for Big Bench to catch the elusive mustang stallion.

Mak left the cottonwood stump and hurried to unfasten the gate for Jim. He tried for a brief reprieve before tomorrow — before Engle got back with his mended jeep.

"Last week when I was looking for Cloud Rise's lost horse," he said, swinging the gate open for Jim, "I caught sight of that wild appaloosa stallion over on the Bench. I can tell you where to track him."

Jim looked down at Mak from his saddle, half amused. "Thanks. Doubt if I'll need your help."

Mak persisted. "It takes more than one rider to bring that one in."

Jim gave a short laugh. "That's partly what bugs me," he said, twisting Mak's meaning. "Too many other riders are out after that award."

"I want to go with you." Mak planted himself in the open gateway.

Nite Boy stood ready in the corral. Hoofs toughened by endless rambles over Makosica, he could cover the rough terrain of Big Bench even better than Jim's wiry little appaloosa mare.

Jim's stirrup brushed Mak's arm lightly as he rode past him.

"Get this straight, Mak. Your job here has nothing to do with wild horses. Your job is to be our choreboy. And to guide our friend Engle to fossils. Wherever they happen to be."

Something like a tiny whip flicked out of Jim Barrack's smoke-blue eyes. They were away from the closeness of horses, back at the beginning with fossils.

"You stick with your job, Mak, and I'll stick with mine. Together, with Dad's help, we may make it. Or do you want to get shed of your part of the bargain?" Jim looked straight down at Mak from his saddle.

Loosa lowered her head just then to nose a horsefly off her extended foreleg.

Between her short stubby ears, Mak caught the slither of a rattlesnake winding itself under a clump of sage a few feet beyond the mare's nose. His thoughts flashed to Gail Barrack's slim moccasined foot idly moving the canvas swing beneath the cottonwood, a stone's throw away.

He whipped the skinning knife from his belt and threw. The blade caught the snake in its middle and pinned it to the sage.

Mak ignored the writhing, bleeding reptile to answer Jim's question. "Don't you say I'm a quitter."

Jim's compact frame loosened in the saddle. "Skip it, Mak. Thought I caught it showing. Guess that rattler scared us both."

Mak said, "I'm not scared of rattlers. I have a way to take care of them."

Jim reached out and gripped Mak's shoulder. "Keep your power working for us, too, will you? It just might get us a wild horse, along with the bones of a mastodon. And help us keep our happy home into the bargain. If that's not asking too much — pard."

"It's not too much."

Then Mak was standing alone at the gate, listening to the diminishing clatter of Loosa's hoofs as she galloped away with Jim in the direction of Big Bench.

The threat of the snake, the overemphasized "pard" talk, had caught him off guard.

Having given his word to Jim Barrack, he had doubled his fear.

Yet, he found comfort in the knowledge that Jim had been driven to reveal a fear of his own — caught showing beneath his easy pretense and self-determination.

Jim was afraid he might lose out against the wild horse.

Jim wouldn't admit he needed help on the horse hunt.

Indian help.

12 "Where Do We Go from Here?"

"Where do we go from here, Mak?"

Dr. Charles Engle nosed his neat red jeep onto the shoulder of the badlands highway at its juncture with the ranch road. He braked it, then waited on the narrow seat for his Indian guide to direct him.

At that moment Mak was wondering what it would be like to get his hands on the jeep's shiny steering wheel. He jerked his eyes from the dashboard and gears to stare at his employer.

"There's only one way to go, sir. That's down the highway into Makosica toward Antelope. The other way leads back across the reservation plains to Whitehorn on the river."

Engle's quick glance swept the vast expanse of the badlands. Where there was everywhere to go. He said, "Jim and I covered the area along the highway to Antelope, Mak. Searching for fossils in road cuts made by highway bulldozers."

"Then we could swing off the highway to Heaven Hill and look around there," Mak suggested. "Heaven Hill's that low ridge about two miles to our right."

"There, too, Mak, Jim and I scouted around for a whole day with no luck. Heaven Hill is mostly sage and sand, with little evidence of sedimentary rock, where fossils usually are found. That is, except for the few stones scattered below it on Scorpion Flats where those deadly scorpions hang out," Engle added with a wry grin.

Mak glanced at the slight, sunburned scientist on the seat beside him. "There's Pinky's Thumb, but that's a hard steep climb," he added, certain that Pinky's Thumb was out even before mentioned.

Through his dark sunglasses Engle measured the bent column of salmon-colored rock that lifted out of the glare of the alkali beds. "You said it, Mak! But what a view from the top!"

"Did you — find any fossils there?" Mak stammered, amazed that the man from college had made the treacherous ascent.

"Nothing but rattlers," Engle answered calmly. "And, of course, that spectacular view of Makosica. Also, I believe Jim caught sight of the wild horse on Big Bench from there. Anyway, he gave one look through my binoculars and said, 'let's go.'" Engle smiled, excusing the young horse rancher's hasty exit from the Thumb. "We may give Pinky's Thumb a more thorough look later on, Mak, in case our other plans fall through."

Mak turned to stare uneasily across the miles of desert wasteland on the opposite side of the highway. Where *did* they go from here, with Engle heading him off on every likely suggestion?

"What's the name of that hogback you're staring at, Mak?" Engle inquired. "I mean the long sharp-edged hump hiding behind the heat haze to our right."

"That's Rattlesnake Ridge," Mak answered, unaware that he'd been staring at anything.

Engle whipped out his binoculars and trained them on the dark, dimly outlined hogback. "Something odd about that land formation," he mused.

"Sure," Mak agreed. "Rocks along the rim make it look like a rattlesnake stretched out there. A boulder uplift makes the head at this end. Rock spill at the other end makes the rattles."

"So I see, but that's not what I mean, Mak. Looks to be of volcanic origin. Different from other formations around here. Igneous rock — that is, rock formed by fire — shows dark, you know. Can't tell, through the heat haze, but — "

Engle lowered his glasses to turn toward Mak. "Just for the fun of it, how far away is Rattlesnake Ridge? As the crow flies, I mean."

Mak smiled. The crow's way was the only way to reach Rattlesnake Ridge. "Six, maybe eight miles. Distance out here fools you."

Those eerie posthole prints were set on the upper slope of Rattlesnake Ridge. And Big Bench, with the canyon wall that held Spirit Face, lay close behind. Engle must be headed off before he got crazy notions "just for the fun of it." "It's a rough trip out there, sir, over gullies and rocky washouts. No trails."

"This jeep is built to cover all kinds of rough terrain, Mak," Engle protested. "The garage boys in Whitehorn have put her in top shape. She'll roll like any army tank over any of your Makosica coulees and boulder-strewn washes." He went back to his binoculars. "Looks like smoke swirling off the top of the ridge."

"That's a whirlwind blowing dust up the sides," Mak said. "Windstorm's building up out there. A man could get lost in it."

That decided it. "You are a tactful guide, Mak," Engle said with a resigned grin. "You are telling me that I am a tenderfoot. That I need to harden up before tackling such ticklish spots in this wild land."

Engle swung the jeep off the ranch road onto the security of the hard-surfaced highway. "After all, I did promise to let you guide me wherever you wish, didn't I?"

"Yes, sir, you did."

"My apology, Mak, for getting carried away. You'll find me forgetful at times. As you suggest, we'll play it safe

79

close to the highway for the present. Recheck some of those cuts gouged out by highway workmen. Who knows, in my last search I may have missed an important find among them. Jim didn't know what to look for. And my own eyesight isn't too good."

The jeep wheeled down the highway in the general direction of Antelope on the eastern edge of Makosica. Mak drew a breath of relief. Engle had let him off, taken the blame. Kept his word.

He chatted sociably now as they drove along, his loose shirt billowing in the hot wind. "Rocks have interested me ever since I was a kid your age. Especially sedimentary rocks — like the walls of the cut we're headed for down the road. There are all kinds of rocks, you know."

Mak didn't know. Up to now, a rock was a rock, useful for throwing at tin-can targets, for killing scorpions and rattlers, or selling to tourists.

Charles Engle halted the jeep at the edge of the highway, pulled the brim of his hat over his eyes, and squinted up the side of the layered embankment.

Mak had ridden Nite Boy through the cut dozens of times. Now he searched the familiar, reddish rock walls as though he, too, never had seen them before.

He recalled how both Engle and Jim had explained about sedimentary rock at the birthday dinner. That it was made up of sand and dead plants and parts of animals, brought together by wind and water, pressed into rock by the great weight of the earth. With the help of minerals and centuries of time.

"Want to take a look?" Engle asked now.

Mak drew back from the proffered binoculars. "No,

thanks, I've looked at all this rock before. When I rode my pony through."

He had no idea what he'd looked at then, or even now. If he used those strange glasses to find out, something in the familiar wall might leap out at him and make him a stranger in his own land.

His employer started the engine. The jeep drifted free of the cut and down the open road.

"When highway workmen made these roads, Mak, their engines and tools exposed some important fossil remains to geologist-paleontologists such as myself. On the other hand, any fossils found in the sedimentary rock of those escarpments beyond us were exposed by the elements rather than by man."

Engle motioned toward the clutter of bare peaks silhouetted indistinctly behind the curtain of heat. "Wind and rain and ice were the tools that eroded the sand overlay to expose any fossils to be found over there. We are prospectors in a way, Mak," he added.

"Pop said the prospectors never found anything worth a darn in Makosica. Except maybe a little black coal dust."

"Perhaps the prospectors looked for the wrong thing," Dr. Engle said. "Wherever men find deposits of sedimentary rock, they are likely to find certain products of the earth far more valuable than all the gold they hunt for. If only rocks could talk, Mak, what a story they would tell! Who knows, your people may have many things of value hidden in the rocks of their Makosica."

"Our medicine men don't tell us that."

"Even so, couldn't some of your younger Indians find strong wa-sic power that says differently?"

"They don't doubt our medicine men." Charles Engle was having a Dream all mixed up with white men's words that Indians could not understand.

The next moment Charles Engle caught sight of an outcrop of rock on the edge of a gully that ran at angles with the highway. "There stands a good example of erosion by wind and water, Mak. That small rough pinnacle that looks like a statue. It's only a stone's throw away. Let's walk over and take a look."

He stopped the jeep on the shoulder of the highway and jumped to the ground.

"That's Indian Rock, sir," Mak said. "It's a good two miles away."

"We'll not take the tool kit, just a chisel and a small hammer. You carry the binoculars, please, Mak." Already the bone man was leaping down the road bank, his heavy boots spraying dust and gravel.

Mak followed with the binocular case slung over his shoulder, his eyes scanning the sun-baked ground for snakes. He was grateful for the protection of the engineer's boots that Engle had brought him from Whitehorn. "I'll take the cost of them out of your first month's wages," he said when Mak protested.

Mak didn't mind that the boots were hot and heavy. They not only protected his feet, they gave him a new importance. Like a partner in a daring business deal.

Engle appeared unaware of any dangers underfoot. He had admitted that he was a tenderfoot, that earlier he had all but let the Makosica desert scare him out. Yet he seemed to take a grim pleasure in defying it. He ignored the alkali dust that swirled up from his boots and caused

82

his sensitive eyes to water. He ignored the cactus that reached out thorns to tear at the legs of his jeans. His eyes were fixed on the statuelike rock ahead of them. He advanced on it, armed with hammer and chisel, like a hungry hunter stalking a fat quarry.

As he strode along, Engle discussed Makosica's rocks as though conversing with an associate in his college geology department.

"Take limestone, now, in relation to shells . . . but then Indian Rock's probably made up of sandstone. Except for that red streak near the base, which could be granite . . . The banks of the gully may be sandstone, which looks like shist, but is stronger. Or would you say they're shale?"

Mak listened, sneezing on dust along with Engle, understanding little, saying nothing.

Out of breath, dripping sweat, they reached the base of Indian Rock. Sandstone, granite, shist, whatever, it had stood crumbling slowly there for ages beneath the fierce and silent sun.

13 Dead Puma at Indian Rock

Indian Rock towered some thirty feet above the rim of the gully. Close up, it looked less like the statue of an Indian and more like an inverted ice cream cone with an oversized cherry balanced on its point.

Charles Engle walked around the base of it, scanning the crumbling walls, leaning back now and then to examine its tip through his binoculars.

"Hold the glasses for me again, Mak. I believe we may have something here."

The paleontologist chipped at a spot in the rocky sides with hammer and chisel. He worked carefully, examining through his hand lens each rocky bit that broke loose. Mak kept a lookout for scorpions that might be clinging to the wall close to Engle's slim, unsuspecting hands.

"Are you digging out a fossil, sir?" he asked at last.

"Not this time," Dr. Engle responded cheerfully. He discarded his collection of broken bits and pocketed his lens. Stepping back from the pinnacle, he took a tube of ointment from his pocket and began to treat the tip of his sunburned nose.

"Actually we don't dig in order to locate fossils, Mak. The fossils will be in plain sight, thanks to weatherwear and highway workmen. After we find them, then we'll dig to get them out. From the looks of the sedimentary rock formations hereabouts, your Makosica should be loaded with fossils."

Mak had sat in on Engle's conversations with Jim. He knew that the geologist spoke from firsthand knowledge of digging for fossils elsewhere in the world. He knew that Engle's books told him about fossils, too. Engle's understanding of fossils made his search for them seem simple and certain.

"You didn't have to dig for your wa-sic, did you, Mak?" he asked to prove his point.

"No." His wa-sic lay on the surface of the earth. And there were walls close beside it, too — frightening walls . . .

Engle waited as if he expected his guide to say more. Mak chose to remain silent.

"Let's go back to the jeep by way of the gully," Engle suggested. "We might find some interesting deposits in the rock along the rim. Seems to be nothing worthwhile at Indian Rock."

They started off along the edge of the gully in the direction of the highway. Alkali sparkled like thick frost on the hot flats ahead of them. In the distance a cavorting whirlwind lifted the white dust, and the sun shining through turned it to gold dust.

"Thar's gold in them there flats." Engle grinned. "White gold. Tons of it."

Let Engle have his joke about gold in Makosica. Mak was more concerned that Engle might fail to find any fossils in the area bordering the highway. And failure would force them deeper inland. No telling where they would wind up. Mak wished he knew more about fossils, how they looked. Where to go to find them. Besides at Spirit Face.

Still not certain what he looked for, Mak caught himself searching the loose rocks that spilled down from the rim of the gully. Some furry thing lay in the scatter of gravel.

Mak stopped short and pointed. "There's a dead puma."

The animal's body lay like a tawny, dust-coated rag, blown along the hot gravel. Its empty eyes were turned toward the fiery rays of the sun.

Mak said, "They can't find food or water. They can't get away from the sun. The heat makes them go crazy. So they die."

Suddenly the drought held a new violence. Engle's glance swept the white-hot horizon that joined with the desperate craving of the land.

"When can we expect rain, Mak?"

"The medicine men don't say."

"Jim tells me that most of the wheat and cattle ranchers around here are dried out," Engle said, as they moved on. "They're deserting the badlands country. Jim thinks the Reeser boys will be next to leave. Obviously it's different with the reservation Indians. Like the puma, they have no other place to go. How do your people make out in times like this, Mak?"

"Superintendent Stoner issues government rations to our old people," Mak said. "The others — well, they've been killing off the tribal herd for meat. They eat their seed wheat."

"But when that's gone?"

"Some of us will go hungry until the rains come." Mak's eyes continued to scan the desert floor ahead of Charles Engle's advancing feet, stumbling and more careless now with heat fatigue. "My people have lived through other droughts. Our medicine men pray and chant for rain, and beg our Father, the Sun, to show mercy. We hold to our Mother, the Earth, who suffers with us."

Engle paused to remove his hat and wipe his sweating forehead. "All well and good to pray. Yet, to a white man like myself, Mak, it seems there should be other more practical ways to help ease the hardship."

Mak stood by, and scuffed the hard-packed earth with the toe of his heavy new boot.

"When I was in Whitehorn to have my jeep repaired," Engle went on, "I talked with some young Indians idling about town — Joe Braids, Al Eagle, Les Bentarm. Know them?"

"I know them."

"The three weren't too friendly about the idea of granting me a permit to dig on Indian land," Engle said.

Mak said cautiously, "Some of the middle-aged Indians and hay farmers might listen better."

"Those young Indians," Engle persisted, "who have nothing to do in times like this — why don't they help their families and locate work in towns and cities off the reservation?"

Mak thought of Les Bentarm, who roamed city streets, got into fights, even went to jail. All for the right to work and live away from the reservation like a white man. The work story of young Indians like Les was deeply bound with race. No white man — not even a sympathetic white man like Dr. Charles Engle — ever could understand that story.

He said simply, "Most of them would rather take their chances with the drought, sir."

"Damn it, Mak!" Engle exploded suddenly. "Can't you think of something else to call me besides *sir?*"

Mak stared at the usually even-tempered man who walked beside him. Had heat got to him — and the thought of hungry Indians, and the sight of the puma, dead of thirst and starvation?

Or was the bone man angry because he failed to find any fossils?

Maybe Engle couldn't face the fact that the wonderful badlands, filled with fossils and other hidden wealth, also held hardship and terror and death.

But Mak still had not answered Engle's question about an appropriate name to call him. Jim and Gail called Dr. Engle Chuck. Mary and Pop had taught Mak to respect his elders, and the familiar nickname hardly seemed proper between an Indian guide and his learned employer.

Engle prodded him irritably for a reply. "We're friends, I hope, Mak."

"Sure, sir — I mean — " Mak broke off, embarrassed at having repeated the disputed word.

Charles Engle halted and looked at his guide across a clump of dried sage. "What's your Indian word for friend, Mak?"

"Our word for friend is *coza.*"

"Well, then?"

Mak stared at the dust-coated toe of his boot. The bone man's fund of knowledge drew him, that and his genuine interest in Indian people. Engle's inexperience with Mak-osica, linked with his determination to reach goals, frightened Mak. But the invitation to friendship had nothing to do with learning or inexperience or goals. It was a thing of the heart, between themselves.

Still, there were others to think of. His fellow tribesmen. To what end might Engle's offer of friendship bind him? In the matter of the permit, for example?

Les Bentarm had warned him at the school gate about "savvying up" to whites . . .

Engle waited for his answer, with the desert sun beating down on his thin pink skin and weak eyes.

Mak stood his ground like the miserable deep-rooted sage that would not give in to drought. Charles Engle began to move on.

"Okay — Coza." Mak gave a shaky grin and lifted his right hand in the sign of the open hand.

Charles Engle nodded, pleased, and returned the sign.

They plodded on, stepping over gopher holes, skirting rocks and sage and tumbleweeds, until they reached the jeep parked at the edge of the highway.

14 Friendly Indian Beadwork

After the day they saw the dead puma at Indian Rock, Charles Engle proceeded as though he expected to find all the fossils he needed near the highway. Mak found an uneasy relief in this.

Repeatedly Engle leaped from the jeep to pounce on some bit of rock that had crumbled from a hillside road cut. He might mention that the knoll from which it fell had stood there for a million years. Then he performed as though a crumb from it might get away the next minute, if he didn't make haste to run it down.

He examined some of the rocks through his pocket lens, then tossed them aside as worthless. He placed others tenderly in the cocoon of his rock kit. These he re-examined under his microscope in the bunkhouse.

"This bit of limestone tells us that your badlands once was a tropical swamp, Mak," he remarked calmly over one such bit of rock.

"How can a little rock tell such a big story as that?" Mak demanded.

"Simply because it carries the imprint of a tiny sea creature called a mollusk. And mollusks of this type are found only in tropical swamps. Want to take a look, Mak?"

Dry dusty Makosica once a hot swamp? Yet there were

those other rocks marked like seashells that he had sold to tourists at Halfway House.

Mak bent his bristly brown head over the microscope while Engle's probe traced a faint, shell-like impression on the magnified rock.

"How come, Coza?"

He looked up from the awesome proof of the bone man's words, expecting Engle to go into the life history of the badlands' mollusk. Dr. Engle had a pleasant way of imparting information to make Mak feel he was being reminded of something he already knew but had forgotten for the moment.

This time instead of explaining, Engle turned to pull a book from the shelf above his bunk. He riffled its pages.

"The writer of this book explains about mollusks far better than I. They began to develop forty million years ago when the earth was mostly rock and slime." He tossed the book on Mak's bunk and turned to work at papers on his desk. "You'll find it good reading," he said.

"It's time for me to do my chores now," Mak said.

He was put out with Coza for expecting him to read for his information. He didn't like books. The books at the Boarding School never told about anything that Indian boys wanted to know.

The book still lay on the bunk when Mak turned in that night. Before returning it to the shelf, he took a quick look into its pages. He was alone in the bunkhouse. Engle was talking with Gail and Jim under the cottonwood across the way. Their voices came through the open bunkhouse door, muted on the cooling night air.

Mak glanced at some of the illustrations and ran

through the captions. Finally the drawing of a mollusk caught his eye. He sank to the edge of the bunk and began to read about it.

Many of the words were foreign and meaningless. Yet he couldn't seem to put the book down. He stumbled through mollusks to dinosaurs, from chicken size to fifty feet long, who disappeared when the swamps disappeared.

"Probably the big ones didn't have the brains to find a different place to live," Mak guessed, pleased that he could relate to a familiar scientific fact. "A pound of brains wouldn't be much help, I guess."

He read on about earth changes that took millions of years, as Engle had said. How gigantic upheavals of rock from the molten core of the earth literally blew up swamps, forming mountains and burying the dinosaurs whose skeletons later became fossils.

The printed pages seemed to hold more than just talk.

Mak read on until the crunch of Dr. Engle's boots in the dooryard roused him. He returned the book to the shelf, snapped off the light, and turned his face to the wall in pretended sleep.

He didn't want to talk the way Coza and he usually talked over the day's work at bedtime. Tonight he had to think.

Tribal legend told that the spirits had caused the bleak peaks and ridges of Makosica. But the white man who wrote Dr. Engle's book said they were formed by forces from the inner earth, then worn down and carved by wind and rain. This book made no mention of spirits wrecking grassland into badlands in order to drive out an enemy.

One of them had to be wrong. The book or the legend.

The book was wrong, of course. It denied the power of his wa-sic. Wa-sic had to come from the spirits as Indian legend told, or everything an Indian wanted in life would be meaningless and lost.

Mak held to his power piece under his blanket and refused to think any other way.

Then in the night his Dream swept through Makosica carrying the fossilized skeleton of a dinosaur. It had a great lashing tail and a tiny foolish head. Mak felt himself lifted from his bunk into the sky to find where it went. He saw his Dream hover above Spirit Face, then drop the skeleton at the spot where he found his wa-sic.

Shaken awake, Mak shot upright in his bunk.

After that there could be no doubt. A whole skeleton of fossils lay hidden at Spirit Face. His wa-sic, and now his Dream, said so.

At midmorning the next day a hot wind leaped wildly out of nowhere to couple its scouring blast with the heat of the sun.

"It's a chinook," Mak said beside Dr. Engle on the seat of the jeep. He bent his strong brown head against the fiery force of it.

The stinging dust swept up from the dried-out land and needled Engle's tender skin without mercy.

"Will the chinook blow up a rain, Mak?"

"No."

"Then with this wind going we may as well return to the bunkhouse. I need a free afternoon, anyway, to report our fossil findings to the Foundation."

Mak wondered what findings Coza meant — aside from

the mollusk and a handful of plant fossils and petrified wood they'd picked up in cuts along the highway.

Later, while Engle was soothing his windburn in the bunkhouse with lotion, Gail called from the kitchen.

"Yoo-hoo, Bone Men. Come and have sandwiches with Mom and me."

Mrs. Barrack laid her crocheting on the windowsill as Mak and Chuck entered the fan-cooled kitchen. She glanced uneasily toward the ominous mist of swirling sand that shrouded Big Bench.

"I wish Jim would give up his horse hunt and get home, too," she said anxiously. "It's not safe for any living thing to be out in that hot blinding duststorm."

Engle and Mak exchanged glances. Each thought of the dead puma at Indian Rock.

"Our chicken sandwiches are skimpy today," Mrs. Barrack apologized at the table. "We've lost two more hens with the heat."

Mak knew that the milch cow had gone dry. The milk and chickens and eggs composed the ranch family's main supply of protein.

Gail's mother managed a smile as she passed a bowl of chokecherry jam. "This blue bowl crossed the plains in a covered wagon," she remarked proudly. "My great-grandmother kept it wrapped in her husband's underwear inside her iron kettle. But it turned out there was no danger from arrows. They happened to be driving through Chief Earth Boy's country. He was friendly to the white people."

Mak looked up quickly over his sandwich. "Chief Earth Boy was Mary Sits' great-grandfather," he said.

"Tell us about him, Mak," Gail begged, pleased with

the friendly link.

"I never knew him." Mak hesitated, then added, "Mary said that Earth Boy could see far with his brain as well as with his eyes. And he knew when it was best to change. That's why he was a great man."

Quietly Mrs. Barrack agreed. "It takes greatness in a man to try for change — especially when he knows everything is against winning. In his own day, at least."

Earth Boy knew his tribe would be exterminated, his cause lost, in seeking to divert the advance of the covered wagons. Did the change he had foreseen lie in another day, in other generations of Indians and whites? Was this what the rancher's wife — and Mary — were trying to tell him about the wisdom of the great chief?

"I wish I could have known Earth Boy," Gail said. After a moment she turned to Chuck. "Speaking of friendly Indians, how would you and Mak like to see my collection of beadwork made by our Indian neighbors? That is, unless you must get to work on your reports right away."

Engle grinned across the table. "What I have to report to the Foundation won't take long, once I get up the nerve to set it down. So cheers for the friendly Indian beadwork!"

Engle's anointed face, his doubtful tone, gave Mak a twinge of guilt. He was to blame because the bone man had so little to report. The Foundation supplied funds for the fossil project. How much longer would such scanty reporting be accepted?

Gail cleared the table for her beadwork and Mrs. Barrack resumed her crocheting beside the window where she could watch for Jim.

"Leave the plates and glasses to wash with the dinner dishes," she told Gail. "It saves on dishwater."

Mak caught the strained anxiety in Gail's face as she left to bring her beadwork. He noticed that the water in the glass pitcher had a cloudy look. They were scraping the bottom of the house well.

Gail brought a covered carton to the table, and began to lift out an assortment of beaded moccasins, fringed buckskin bags, pipes, neckties, dance ornaments. She named the maker of each piece — Serena Songbird, Ruth Weaselhead, Mary Moses, Deborah Deerhorn . . .

"You know who made this, Mak." Gail smiled as she held up a beaded buckskin shoulder piece, heavily fringed with dyed porcupine quills.

"I remember it," he said. Was it only last summer that he had hunted the porcupine, watched Mary's strong hands scrape and soften the deer hide, her clever fingers design the beaded pattern?

A lump came in his throat at thinking how quickly his way of life had changed since he left the hot little lean-to kitchen at Halfway House and Mary's smoke-stained tepee on the crest of the coulee. Now he sat at a wide family table with its cloth rippled coolly by an electric fan; he couldn't resist reading books about the awesome reshaping of his Mother, the Earth; he whizzed down the highway in a neat red jeep beside a paleontologist who searched Makosica for skeletons of animals believed to have lived there millions of years ago . . .

"Here's another prize piece," Gail was saying of a buckskin vest. Its solidly beaded front of pale blue and white

96

and green also was familiar to Mak.

"That's Cloud Rise's war-dance vest!" he exclaimed, recalling the old Indian with the black glasses whose lost horse had led him to his wa-sic.

"Right," said Gail. "Cloud Rise's wife made him a new vest, so she traded me the old one for Reddie, my yearling steer."

Mak clapped his hand over his mouth in the Indian sign of surprise. "A yearling steer for that worn-out old vest?" he exclaimed.

"Amy Cloud Rise needed meat to feed her family," Gail said simply. She went on with her showing.

"Many Camps traded this beaded belt to Dad for a shovel," she told Engle. "And Bessie Blackbird left her husband's hatband in exchange for two loaves of Mom's fresh bread."

When Engle had examined the elegant native men's wear, Gail lifted a beaded leather bag from the box. "George Arrow traded me this bag for my locket. George wanted the locket for his bride. It was a little tarnished, anyway," she added as though to minimize her parting with the treasured bit of jewelry.

The ranch girl smiled to herself as, finally, she took up a pair of child's moccasins from the box. "I started my collection with these little moccasins when I was five years old," she said. "By that time I'd switched from trikes to horses. So I traded my trike to Allie Gun's little boy for his new moccasins. He pulled them off and practically threw them at me to claim the trike," she recalled with a laugh.

At the window, Mrs. Barrack laughed along with Gail. "The chinook's dying down," she announced, glancing off over the badlands.

At the table Charles Engle gave Gail enthusiastic praise for her Indian beadwork. "A valuable collection you have here. You've sacrificed a lot to acquire it. What do you plan to do with it?"

She said, "I have an offer from a collector in Denver who wants to buy it — when it's completed."

"Great! How much more do you need?"

"Actually, I need only one more piece — a chieftain's headdress." She gave a little sigh. "Indian headdresses are hard to come by. Not many of the old war chieftains are alive. Indian families treasure the headdresses that are left, to hand down to their children."

Mak thought how proudly and jealously Mary Sits had guarded her Great-grandfather Earth Boy's headdress in her tepee beside Halfway House. He remembered its luxurious sweep of eagle feathers, the richness of weasel tails and shiny strings of dyed porcupine quills.

Gail argued with herself as she returned the beadwork to the box. "Even if I could locate a headdress," she said, "I have nothing more to trade, no more steers or jewelry. I own Paint, of course. But he's been mine since he was born. He's part of my family. Anyway," she concluded practically, "I'm still in high school. College is a long way off. I have lots of time to find a headdress."

She looked up, aware that Chuck and Mak had no idea what lay behind her words. She hastened to explain. "You see, I expect to use the money from my beadwork collection to train as a teacher. There's talk of a school-house being built for ranch kids and Indian kids on the school section north of our place. I plan to teach there some day when that school is built."

Mak knew about the school section and the school that never materialized. He caught the determination in Gail Barrack's voice, which left no doubt that she intended to carry her plan through. She came from a line of determined women. They had faced harsh change and brought delicate china in covered wagons to new homes in the badlands country.

Mrs. Barrack's relieved voice roused Mak from his thoughts.

"There comes Jim now!" She leaned forward to stare through the window. "What's that he's carrying over his saddle, Mak?"

At her shoulder, Mak said, "Looks something like a dead colt."

He hurried from the kitchen ahead of the others to open the ranch gate for Jim.

15 The Colt

The limp body of a newborn colt lay across Jim Barrack's saddle like a dirty fur rug.

"He's not dead," Jim told Mak defiantly above his quiet burden. "Tell Gail to bring some warm milk in a bottle.

Don't stand there and stare like a dope! *Get going!*"

Just then Jim saw Gail start from the kitchen with her mother and Chuck Engle close behind. "Get me some warm milk, Gail," he yelled.

Mak rushed from the gate to spread a blanket on the straw in the empty calf pen. Jim scared him the way he sagged in the saddle, red-eyed and powdered with dust, barking out hoarse orders.

At the barn Mak stood by while Jim laid the body of the colt gently on the blanket. Its staring eyes were filmed with dust from the searing chinook. Its dark hair, damp and matted by birth, was coated with dust clods.

Jim yanked off his neck scarf and thrust it toward Mak. "Wet it at the tank."

Jim laid the cool sopping scarf over the colt's eyes to soothe them. He looked down at the colt, hands clenched, legs braced as though set for a fight.

"He's got good blood in him," Jim said. "He was sired by the appaloosa mustang."

To Mak, the colt looked as though he had no blood at all in him.

Chuck Engle asked, "How did you happen to find him?"

Jim's answer was slow, groping, as if he sought to transfer a small miracle into a purpose of his own.

"The chinook wore me down and I headed for home. At the rim of the Bench I heard the colt's faint whinny from an outcrop of boulders. I rode back. He'd got away from the mare and was trapped among the boulders. The mare was nowhere around. He was only a few hours old — too weak from lack of food to stand. The pumas would have got him before morning. Anyway . . ."

Jim grasped the bottle of milk as Gail came up with it. He dropped beside the still creature on the blanket and lifted its limp head to his knee. He forced the colt's mouth open and squeezed drops of warm milk from the bottle onto its dry pink tongue.

"Rub his throat, Gail. We want to get some of this milk down your gullet, Chinook Boy," he said to the seemingly lifeless animal.

The wild colt couldn't drink. Jim coaxed, and tried again.

Mrs. Barrack brought coffee.

"Thanks, Mom. I've got to save him."

"Of course, Jim."

Jim took turns between trying to feed the colt and gulping coffee. He probed at dust balls that clogged the delicate nostrils, he rubbed the knobby legs and fawn-sized feet.

Suddenly he looked up at the others as though surprised to find them standing there. "Beat it, you guys," he said. "Thanks, but you can't do anything. This is up to me."

Mak followed Gail out of the cow barn and across the corral toward the house. Nite Boy and Paint turned from the watering tank to stare at them. The paint, his creamy hide blotched with exotic masses of brown, nickered softly at the girl. Gail gave a skipping run, then a jump, and landed on his back. She swung off on the opposite side and threw her arm about the pony's creamy neck. She stood there a moment, with her cheek pressed to his, crooning to him.

Nite Boy tossed his head and backed away from them.

Gail gave a shaky laugh. "Indian ponies can't stand soft stuff. Even so, you and Nite Boy think a lot of one another, too, don't you, Mak?"

She was upset about the plight of the wild colt, Mak could tell. She made talk to keep from crying. He went along with her. "Nite Boy gets me places," he admitted.

"It's more than that," she insisted. "He whinnies after you when you drive off with Chuck. I think he's jealous of the jeep. Sometimes I ride him around the pasture for a little while to keep him from getting lonesome," she confessed. "And to get him used to me."

"He doesn't know anything about girls," Mak said. "But you can ride him whenever you want," he offered.

"Thanks. But then, that makes Paint jealous." She stroked her pony's face. The paint closed his glassy eyes and lowered his head to receive her attention. "Paint and I never have been separated since the night he was born," Gail said. "I think more of him than anything I have."

Mrs. Barrack called from the kitchen door. "Mom wants me to help with dinner. Grain them, Mak, will you?" Gail turned to go. "Give each of them an extra helping."

Mak hesitated. She knew that Jim had put a stop to extra helpings for the ponies, with oats running low in the bin.

"Just this once," she begged.

"Okay." He took his chance against Jim and humored her. He guessed he did it because of the little wild colt in the calf pen.

Later at the bunkhouse, Charles Engle said, "Think he'll live, Mak?"

"I never saw a colt so far gone."

"Jim's already named him. The way he talked, he's pinning his hopes for breeding stock on that wild colt."

Mak nodded. He thought he knew what Charles Engle meant. Should the appaloosa mustang on Big Bench be captured, or dead, the prize money was lost. All that would be left to Jim as a breeder of appaloosa horses lay in this pitiful remnant of horseflesh the wild mustang had sired.

A sorry hope. But with Jim, when he lost out one way, he set himself to win another way. Jim Barrack meant to hang in there with a half-dead colt.

Mak drew a slow deep breath. Jim refused his help on the horse hunt, caught his fear showing, called him a dope. Jim never gave up.

If he ever had a big brother, Mak guessed he'd want him to be like Jim.

"There's that Rattlesnake Ridge again, Mak, hunkering down among all those eroded formations."

It was late afternoon. They were spinning down the highway toward the eastern boundary of the Montana badlands.

Beneath the lowering sun, the land lay stretched out parched and rigid in its wait for rain. The chants of holy tribesmen so far had been in vain. No cloud moved in the sky to give Mak a sign, no animal, not even a bird alerted him. No sign of fossils, either. Even with strong wa-sic, Mak felt helpless and defeated.

"What's over there besides rattlers, Mak?"

"On Rattlesnake Ridge? Nothing much, I'd say."

Except for those posthole prints that came from nowhere and led nowhere. It annoyed Mak that he had to be reminded of them.

Engle halted the jeep in the middle of the highway to turn his binoculars once again on the sharply rimmed hogback beyond them.

"There's a lot more than the head and the tail to that ridge, Mak. It's no uplift. From here it looks like part of a lava flow. The corded type of lava. I can see the series of hardened ridges on the sides. A lava formation seems out of place in this land of sedimentary rock."

"Think there's any fossils over there?" Mak dared entertain a latent hope, even with Spirit Face close behind the ridge.

"No, Mak. A lava flow consists of melted rock that boils up out of the center of the earth. Any prehistoric animals caught in it were incinerated — that is, burned up — leaving little or no evidence of themselves."

"No use to go there then," Mak said. "Sometimes I don't understand the things you say about Makosica," he blurted. "Or the words I read about it, either."

Sometimes the waves of heat that shimmered across Makosica made it look like a steaming swamp.

Sometimes the land he knew so well seemed to rise and fall beneath the wheels of the jeep in response to the jar of unknown forces deep inside it.

It was Engle's talk that mixed him up. And Engle's books.

Charles Engle caught a guarded hungering beneath the impatience in his guide's voice. "Okay, Mak, shoot. What are some of the words that bother you?"

Mak made stumbling pronunciation. Liquid core, glaciation, diastrophic . . .

"All are simple words relating to earth change," Engle assured Mak lightly. "Take that word diastrophic." Engle slowed the jeep to drifting speed and relaxed against the back of the seat. "Diastrophic forces are movements inside the earth that fold and twist rocks and lift great masses of them through the earth's crust to change it."

"The only crust I really know about is pie crust." Mak joked to ease the seriousness of his need to know more.

Engle grinned. "The earth's crust is twenty miles thicker — and a lot tougher — than the crust Mrs. Barrack makes."

A sweep of his arm took in the peaks and ridges scattered over the floor of the badlands — Pinky's Thumb, Ghost Ridge, Heaven Hill. "Those formations are some of the giant blocks thrust out of the earth by diastrophic forces, Mak. In turn they have been changed by other forces that eat at them and wear them down."

"By erosion, you mean," Mak said from his new book-reading.

"Right — the weathering by wind and water and ice, as far back as the age of glaciers. Our wonderful Mother, the Earth, never stays the same, Mak. She changes constantly." Engle smiled at Mak from across the narrow seat. "As you have read, it's these marvelous processes of change — the building up and tearing down — that expose the fossils we're after."

Building up . . . tearing down . . . marvelous change . . .

Something inside Mak warned him of the danger of

knowing too much about change. Any kind of change.

"We waste so much time with talk about change we forget to look for fossils," he reminded his employer shortly.

"It's time we turned back home, anyway," Engle said. "We've found about all there is to find along the highway. Isn't that the town of Antelope ahead of us at the eastern edge of the badlands?"

"Right." Mak glanced across the caldron of the land to a handful of cabins, scattered like bleached bones along a sandy slope.

Mary Sits lived in one of those cabins with her sister. Mak could picture Mary's serene bulk bent over beadwork in her new leaf arbor, pausing now and then to show her nieces and nephews how to write their names in the dust. He seemed to hear her singsong voice droning out legends. How Coyote, the song dog, found his song. How Buffalo got his hump. Where Eagle nested in the crags. Sacred animals, put here for a purpose, having equal rights with human beings.

He was shaken by a wave of homesickness and helplessness, promptly jolted out of him as Engle turned the jeep about on two wheels and headed homeward in a scud of gravel dust.

He must no longer let himself think of childhood things. A week of exploring along the highway had come to an end with nothing gained except a handful of miscellaneous fossils. Further search must move inland. Farther inland, even, than Rattlesnake Ridge.

Already Mr. Barrack had returned from Whitehorn to spend his first weekend with his family, then resumed his work at the garage in town. Concern over the sick colt left little time for family discussion about the fossil hunt. Mak dreaded their questions, yet total lack of interest worried him even more.

He had given his word, on their doorstep, to guide Engle to fossil remains. His job, his home and theirs depended on keeping his word. Coza had offered him a generous week on trial. He had wasted it stalling for time.

16 Winds of Change

They turned off the highway into the ranch road with the fast-setting sun in their faces.

Engle returned to their conversation.

"The way I see it, Mak, our talk about earth change isn't exactly wasted. Understanding about changes in our earth helps us to change, too. Wouldn't you say that's good?"

The lowering sun-rays gave a false flush of life to the cheek of distant Ghost Ridge. Beside the spinning wheels of the jeep a rosy glow livened the gray skeletons of roadside chokecherry, and etched a new beauty to dead clumps of tumbleweed and buffalo peas.

Mak tossed Engle's question back. "You mean that getting acquainted builds us up and tears us down — like the earth. And that's good?"

"In a way, yes," his friend replied. "As we get to know one another, we exchange ideas that break through the crust of our former beliefs. Erosion of old beliefs changes the way we think and feel and act. And as we change, we grow.

"Take myself, for example. Since I've come to know you, Mak, I've changed my understanding of your people. I had supposed it would be simple to obtain a permit for excavating fossils on Indian land. That meeting in Whitehorn with your three friends, Joe Braids, Al Eagle, and Les Bentarm, changed my mind, because I began to understand Indian reasons for not wanting to allow it."

Mak wondered what kind of big talk Les Bentarm had given Coza about the permit. Les and his followers wouldn't have the whole say about the permit, anyway.

Mak caught himself. What had come over him that he should think to side with a white man against his fellow tribesmen?

He put Engle on the spot. "Do you believe, Coza, that the Indian people also might change their minds about wanting to give you the permit?"

"Yes, given time and certain circumstances. It takes time, Mak, to build up mountains. Time to wear them down."

What "certain circumstances" did Coza mean, that could cause his people — the Earth People — to change; to agree with a white man who wanted to take from their sacred land?

Coza was smart, but for all his confidence he was wrong if he believed that.

They jolted down the rutted road toward the ranch. Before they arrived, Mak had to get this matter of change straight with himself.

"Okay, Coza, my land has changed. You have changed. You believe my people can change. Will I change, too?"

Engle smiled over the steering wheel. "You've already changed to reading science books in the evening, haven't you, instead of playing checkers with Gail, or chewing the fat with Jim and me?"

"So *how* has reading the books changed me?"

"For one thing Mak, it has you asking me, a white man, questions about your own Mother, the Earth."

They were sparring with words, close to the root of his problem. He brought it out into the open.

"These answers you and your books give me about my Earth Mother. Do you think they build me up so that I will wear down the thinking of my ancestors and use my white man's eyes to find the way to your fossils?"

If Charles Engle caught the native disdain behind his guide's question, he gave no sign. "The answers I give to your questions only point out directions, Mak. It's up to you to make the choices."

Mak moved irritably on the seat beside Engle. Coza talked like Pop, who raised him to know what was right and best "so as you can make your own choice."

Sure, life was different for him now. He was part of a rancher's family. He ate like them, worked with them, hoped for the same things. But at heart he remained Indian. Chief Earth Boy never meant there was a time when

109

an Indian should change from being Indian.

They reached the ranch gate. The jeep turned in and came to a halt in the dooryard.

Mak jumped out and slapped his mouth into a loud war whoop. The weird, wild sound of it set Yaller into startled barking at the doorstep.

Gail came laughing from the house. "Yaller and I thought we heard a wild Indian whooping at our gate, but it was only you, Mak."

Mak looked straight at her. "I am Indian. I'm telling the world. My blood's divided but inside me I'm all Indian. I don't change."

"And that's what I like about you, too, Mak," she returned warmly. "That you keep yourself Indian."

Charles Engle gave Mak a little salute, then hurried to the bunkhouse to check on the day's mail.

Mak turned to unload the jeep.

Gail said quietly, "Cloud Rise dropped by to see you, Mak."

"Cloud Rise? What did he want?"

Gail smiled. "First he gave me some soft talk about his good friend, Makosica Mike. How you found his Shunga-toga at Big Bench where some kind of evil spirit wouldn't let anyone else go. Did I understand him right?"

Almost right to the fossil spot. "What did Cloud Rise want?"

"He brought a message from your Mother Woman. Wouldn't that be Mary Sits?"

"What does Mary want?" Mak demanded. It wasn't like Mary to be sending messages about unimportant things. Was Mary sick?

A faint frown wrinkled the girl's forehead. "Cloud Rise came to say that Mary wants you and Chuck to come to the Dogtown powwow below the Agency."

"When?" The muscles in Mak's throat tightened.

"Cloud Rise made the sign for the sun, like this." Gail formed an incomplete circle with her index finger and thumb. She held it toward the east, then lowered it in a curve toward the west. Next she indicated the numeral two by extending the third and fourth fingers of her right hand while holding the first two down with her thumb. "Two suns away, or day after tomorrow. Friday, wouldn't that be?"

"Yes, Friday." Mak was surprised at Gail's ability to understand the Indian sign language. She had gained more than beadwork from the Indians when she bought their handiwork at Halfway House.

"Did Cloud Rise say why Mary wants Coza and me at the Dogtown Council Meeting on Friday?"

"Something about a white paper that Chuck needs from the Indians. A permit to dig for fossils, wouldn't it be?"

Mak stood staring at the ground as though to think.

"Chuck has said he needs permission from the Tribal Council to dig for fossils," Gail went on. "But why the rush? Couldn't the permit come later? I mean, you and Chuck haven't found any fossils yet. Or have you?"

Mak caught a breathless hesitation beneath her words. "Not yet. Not many."

"Well, you still have tomorrow to look," she said.

Mak turned to unfasten Engle's empty canteen, strapped to the side of the jeep. "Sure," he said. "We still have tomorrow. Today's only Wednesday."

111

His fingers fumbled with the strap of the canteen. "How's the colt?" he asked as though, after all, the colt was the most important thing to be considered around the ranch.

She stooped to fondle Yaller. His volley of joyous barks at finally being noticed eased the tension. They laughed at him.

"Chinook Boy's begun to drink milk now," Gail told Mak. "That leaves Jim free to ride off on the horse hunt again. He's out in the calf pen with the colt now, if you want to see him."

"Right now I have to unload the gear," Mak said.

He couldn't face Jim Barrack across the calf pen, not with only one day to even up ten days of failure. He couldn't take Mary's message to Coza, with only a paltry showing of fossils on which to base his claim for a permit.

He had to get away somewhere, anywhere, to think about tomorrow. To some place like the cave with the writing on its walls, hidden in the bank of the coulee below Halfway House.

There he had worked off boyish rebellion against mopping the lunchroom floor. Or returning to the Boarding School when he wanted to search for his wa-sic.

He had loosened his frustrations with blood-curdling hunter yells while he fired his slingshot at masses of rolling tumbleweeds, pretending they were the long-lost buffalo. At the mouth of the cave he had made smoke signals to alert other imagined scouts when to attack white men in covered wagons who swept in hordes across Indian land ... Until a great chieftain, who knew when it was time to change, called off his warriors.

He was only a kid then, with only small troubles.

Yet, as he checked the picks and shovels strapped to the side of the red jeep, Mak longed for that childhood haven where he could get straight with himself.

17 Think About Tomorrow

When Mak finished unloading the jeep, Gail followed him to the corral tank, where he pumped water for Nite Boy and the milch cow.

"I meant to tell you, Mak," she began casually, as though it had slipped her mind until that moment, "Cloud Rise told me where I can find a chieftain's headdress for my collection."

Mak looked at her quickly from across the water tank. "Whose?"

"Old Walking Crane's."

She stood beside Nite Boy, twisting the stiff black hairs of his mane around her fingers while he drank, not looking at Mak.

Mak knew Walking Crane; wizened, self-important, an early-day camp crier. The old fullblood still took it upon himself to strut about the Agency in his war regalia, announcing celebrations and Council meetings, often to the amusement of the younger Indians.

Mak said, "Walking Crane's war bonnet is made of turkey feathers."

Gail ignored his slighting comment. "Cloud Rise said that Walking Crane is sick. He won't go to the government doctor at the Agency Hospital. Says his own medicine will cure him. His granddaughter, Evangeline Redrock, is worried. She has to sell Walking Crane's headdress for money to buy food and supplies for him."

Gail's words tumbled over themselves. She drew a quick breath and added lightly, "Anyway, I thought I'd ride over there tomorrow and take a look at the headdress. Jim's going to use Loosa on the horse hunt so I'll need Paint, Mak. Will you ride Nite Boy over to Reeser's pasture and bring Paint in for me? This evening?"

When drought forced the Reeser boys to leave the badlands country, Jim had turned Paint into their vacant pasture. Grass wasn't eaten down as closely there as on Barrack Ranch and Reeser's pasture had a waterhole with a spring. The change to better feed relieved Gail, who worried about the way her pony's ribs and hip bones had begun to show.

"You don't have to ride Paint to Redrock's place. You can ride Nite Boy. He needs a good workout, anyway. Since I travel by jeep these days," Mak added with a grin.

He was talking around whatever it was that compelled Gail to part with her pony for Walking Crane's headdress to complete her beadwork collection.

"I know I can ride Nite Boy, but I want Paint," Gail said. The finality in her voice had a hollow ring.

114

Mechanically Mak worked the pump handle up and down. Beside the water tank Yaller scratched his ear, groaning gently with the pleasure of it. Nite Boy went on drinking in long wheezing sucks.

"Please, Mak."

It was four miles to Reeser's gate. He was tired and hungry, thinking over his talk with Engle, worried about the Council summons. But it wasn't that. He liked doing things for Gail. He didn't want her to think he was trying to get out of it. Paint was her pony. She could do what she chose with him. He was only the Indian choreboy, hired help.

He stepped around the corner of the water tank. He swung himself over Nite Boy's back and slapped his rump. With his body, Mak guided the wiry little black out of the corral and galloped off toward the Reeser place.

Taken by surprise at Mak's sudden action, Gail called after him. "I don't mean right now, Mak. Eat your dinner first."

But Mak didn't seem to hear. He had to get off by himself.

The sun dropped behind the badlands country in a blaze of fiery triumph. Soon a cool pearly twilight would take over for a few hours until the ruthless sun-power returned to sear the land for another day.

Mak dismounted Nite Boy at Reeser's gate. He turned his black pony into the pasture and refastened the gate.

Boy and pony stared at one another across the barbed-wire fence. Now that he'd done this thing, Mak seemed as surprised as Nite Boy. But he wasn't about to make it possible for Gail Barrack to sacrifice her beloved pony for that crummy turkey-feather headdress. Because that was why she wanted Paint. He could stop it by keeping both ponies out of her reach.

It would be a rough walk under tomorrow's sun to get Paint from Reeser's pasture. Even a gritty girl like Gail Barrack would not risk sunstroke.

"Beat it," Mak shooed Nite Boy away. "Go find Paint. He's off somewhere in Reeser's hills."

Desert earth cooled first in the depressions, and Mak sought a deep draw to begin the long walk home. The night air released final traces of scent from the Indian musk struggling to grow there.

He pulled a handful of the withered stalks, remembering how he had gathered musk for Mary to scent her hair. He longed to be with Mary again, with his own people. Not separate and apart as now. He would see Mary and the others, of course, day after tomorrow at the Dogtown Council Meeting on the river below the Agency. But that wouldn't be a happy time. It could be a serious matter to stand before the tribunal of his people with a white man who asked to take from Indian land.

He was alone, quieted down in the cool desert darkness. His thoughts cleared.

It would make no difference to the Tribal Council whether Coza presented a handful of fossils or an entire fossilized mastodon skeleton. *The Indians wanted nothing at all to be taken from their sacred land by white men.* Their concern was based on legendary respect for their Mother, the Earth. This ancient Indian belief would not change "under certain circumstances" as Coza had said.

Why then his urge to swell Coza's findings before Friday night? Why should he divide himself from his people with muddled thinking?

The June moon lifted like a pale bubble on the horizon. Far off in Makosica a coyote called. The song dog's weird howl held a sound of betrayal. Mak covered his ears to shut it out.

When tomorrow came, he would have no answers. As a paid guide, he would go through the motions of another search, wherever it led. Even though there was little chance of finding a way to convince the Council in Coza's favor. Still counting on his wa-sic to see him through. If it was strong enough.

If? Was he beginning to doubt his power, too?

Mak lingered with the morning chores, dreading to meet Gail at breakfast.

Loosa's stall was empty. Before he rode her off to Big Bench, Jim had fed Chinook Boy. Even so, the little colt nickered greedily at sight of Mak. The tiny animal's voice was strong and hoarse, although his legs still were weak. After a tangled struggle to stand, he dropped back on the straw and stared at Mak out of white-rimmed eyes.

Gail looked up over the toaster when finally Mak appeared for breakfast. She gave him her usual greeting — the sign of the open hand. The friendly gesture only made it harder for Mak to tell her what he had to say.

He returned the sign and laid some sprigs of dried musk clumsily at her plate. He pulled out his chair. "I didn't bring Paint back last night. Or Nite Boy, either."

117

She rolled a stalk of musk between her palms and rubbed the scent over her hair, the way Mary did it.

"I guess I didn't expect you to, Mak." She added, "I heard Jim ride Loosa off for Big Bench at daybreak. So that leaves me grounded — at least for another day."

A glint of defiance in her eyes made him helpless to defend his stand against trading Paint for Walking Crane's headdress. He was relieved to hear Engle speak from the doorway.

"What's this about Jim riding off to Big Bench again, Gail?"

She broke eggs in a skillet. "If one appaloosa is going to live, two would be better — providing the second one still is alive, of course. Jim's got to find out for himself. All of which leaves me holding the bottle!"

"You both have my blessing." Chuck grinned, seating himself at his usual place. "Where's your mom?" he asked, noting that Mrs. Barrack's chair was empty.

Gail set buttered toast and the platter of fried eggs before them. "Mom doesn't feel very well this morning. I guess it's the heat. Coffee?"

Mak thought, bent over his plate, that hardy little Mrs. Barrack would be the last to give in to heat.

Engle held up his empty cup. "Please." While waiting for her to serve him, he inquired, "I heard you talking over the telephone to your father yesterday. Everything okay at the garage?"

She stood holding the coffee pot, her back turned, saying nothing.

"Something wrong, Gail?"

Still without turning she shook her lowered head no.

"Has your father been laid off at the garage?" Engle persisted gently.

She brushed her hand across her eyes and nodded assent, her head turned away. "Why doesn't it rain?" she choked.

Engle went to her with the empty cup. "Pour it for your mother. I'll take care of Mak's and mine."

Mak heard her leave the kitchen with the coffee, his eyes on his plate.

So that was why Gail needed to trade Paint for Walking Crane's headdress. So she could sell her completed collection for funds to help keep the ranch going, because her father had lost his job.

She had tried to spare him the bad news, even as she knew that he alone held the way to make her sacrifice unnecessary. She liked his cowlick, his war whoop, and she liked him because he kept himself Indian.

Now he was letting her down for a reason so deeply Indian that it couldn't be explained or denied.

18 Sky Picture

"Got your compass, Coza?"

Engle pounded his pants pocket. "Check." He grinned triumphantly, having forgotten his compass twice before. He stepped into the jeep, taking the seat that Mak usually occupied.

Mak waited for him to slide under the steering wheel. His friend had remembered his compass, but had he forgotten where he sat?

"You're the driver from now on, Mak," he said lightly. "It's my turn to enjoy the scenery."

Mak walked around the back of the jeep and slipped slowly under the steering wheel. For days he had itched to get his hands on the wheel of the sturdy little rig, but now that it was his to control he felt afraid of it.

Was it because of the scenery? Or did Engle figure it was about time — with Mr. Barrack out of work — that his Indian guide got down to the business of carrying through his job?

Mak started the jeep with a jerk and drove it out of the ranch gate, barely missing the post. Not knowing where he was headed.

Nothing had been said, either by Gail or himself, about the summons to the Tribal Council. He'd tell Coza when the right time came.

Outside the ranch gate Engle grasped Mak's arm. "Hold it, Mak! There's a mirage rising over the badlands. Talk about scenery!"

Mirages in the badlands were nothing new to Mak Malloy. He shot an uneasy glance toward the eastern horizon.

"It's a sky picture," he said. He started to drive on, but again Engle stopped him. "What a sight!" he breathed.

Invisible giant hands seemed to be pulling the blue mass of the badlands away from the body of the surrounding plains. They wrenched off a layer of peaks and benches, picked them up, and left them free to float in the sky. There they were stretched into tremulous shapes that looked like ruins of ancient cities. Layers of color, wavering from blue to pink, sifted like mist through imaginary domes and pillars. Below them new shapes began to move and take form, to be lifted in turn as those before them melted away in the sky. An arresting and earth-shattering holocaust performed in ghostly silence.

Engle grasped his binoculars to bring the spectacle closer. Remembering Mak, he thrust the glasses across the seat. "Take a look," he invited excitedly.

Mak shook his head. "Thanks, but I don't like to look at sky pictures."

"Why not?"

"They are a bad sign from the spirits."

Engle continued to drink in the eerie sight through his powerful lenses. "I seem to see the mirage differently from you, Mak," he remarked after a moment. "I see it as a phenomenon of Nature, caused by the bending of light rays as they pass through different layers of air. Thick air, thin air, hot or cool air. From a distance the reflections appear to lift the top right off the land into the sky. That's what makes it seem unreal to us."

"Have you read all that in your books?" Mak asked in curious defiance.

"Up to now I've had to read for information about the mirage," Engle admitted. "But today I have the experience of actually living through the wonder of it. This is one of the most awesome sights I've seen in all Nature, Mak."

Mak found a grim satisfaction in knowing a homeland spectacle, frightening as it was, that was unfamiliar to the learned man from college.

He fastened his eyes on the dry ruts of the ranch road and sat stiffly while his companion continued to stare through his glasses at the colorful display in the sky.

Engle and his books and his college couldn't be right about everything. That strange twisting together of land and sky had to be something other than mere light and air.

Sky pictures came from the spirits as a warning. Warning of danger in heeding the talk and writings and the work of white men.

The mirage began to fade away. Dr. Engle returned his binoculars to their case. The fantasy was gone, the kingdom of desert drought and desolation re-established once more.

"Okay, Mak, let's go."

Mak fed gas and the jeep lurched forward down the ranch road. He still didn't know where he was headed. Right now his one thought was to put the spirits of the sky picture — and Engle's interpretation of them — behind him.

The mirage had caused a little island of silence to settle on the car seat between them.

Finally Mak broke into it.

"You don't believe in spirits, do you, Coza?"

"Yes, I do, Mak. I believe in the spirit of love, the spirit of truth, the spirit of God."

"But you don't believe in the spirits of the sky picture," Mak persisted over the steering wheel.

Charles Engle answered honestly. "I don't believe that spirits have anything to do with a mirage, Mak. Such thinking would not be in accord with known laws of science. In my opinion the spirits you mention belong in the category of charms, omens, the supernatural, and superstition."

Superstitious nonsense . . . Mak could not accept Engle's explanation. "I prayed to the Great Spirit to give me my wa-sic power, and you seem to believe in that."

"I believe in a power that guides the heart and will of each of us. Call it what you choose."

Mak drove the jeep off the ranch road into a dry shallow wash that angled cross-country into the desert wilderness.

He wouldn't try to figure it out. Let his wa-sic take over for him. That was what he risked his life for, wasn't it — guidance by his power?

The jeep careened along the pebbly bottom of the draw. Engle grasped his hat with one hand and the edge of the seat with the other. "Where are we headed in such a hurry?"

Mak glanced across the maze of buttes and flats all around them. Rattlesnake Ridge loomed straight ahead.

Its long brown rim was outlined like a giant prehistoric viper against the white-hot sky.

He measured the dark ominous crouch of it. "You want to see Rattlesnake Ridge because it's lava rock and different from the others. So why don't we go there? We could see some strange marks I found there, and mix them with things we read in books. Maybe they will come out to be fossils."

Engle shot his guide a cautious glance. "The ghosts of history make strange marks," he said, "but can prehistoric animals leave their bones in igneous rock, formed by fire, Mak?"

Of course they couldn't. The books, and Engle, and even his common sense told him that. The animals' bones would have been destroyed in the molten lava. In his headlong haste to escape the spirits of the sky picture he was cornered by his own rash game of words.

Stubbornly he countered, "I have wa-sic that can work strong power against ghosts, Coza."

Beside him Charles Engle squinted thoughtfully at Rattlesnake Ridge, its brown bulk drawing closer now. "There may have been an advance of animals before the lava flow," he reflected. "So you could be right, Mak. Your wa-sic might lead us to some fossilized remains at Rattlesnake Ridge. Near the base of the ridge where the flow stopped, I mean."

Coza had an irritating way of twisting matters about, so they seemed promising and simple when everything was complicated and hopeless.

Mak began to relax a little at the steering wheel.

19 Fossil Find

Draws and coulees and boulder-strewn washes slashed the alkali flats like spaces between spread fingers. True to Engle's boast the jeep rolled like an army tank over them all. Mak found release in the sturdy power beneath his hands as he gripped the steering wheel.

Engle sneezed when a cloud of alkali dust enveloped them. Gypsum, he called it.

"There's enough gypsum around here to stock half the cement plants, fertilizer plants, and chemical plants — in the entire United States." He broke off with a cough. "Pity that such valuable chemicals must go to waste," he added, sneezing again.

"Fertilizer for what?" Mak asked, his eyes glued to the rough way-the-crow-flies to Rattlesnake Ridge.

"Fertilizer to grow crops and grass for lawns and parks and golf courses."

Mak found other things to think of besides white-man notions about fertilizers for golf courses.

Mary would be sitting on the Council tomorrow night. How would she look at Engle's request to dig on Mako-sica?

He never could be sure what stand Mary would take. She steeped him in the legends of their people, then urged his schooling like white boys'. And found him a home with a white man's family.

Because Mary was a great-granddaughter of Chief Earth Boy, her word carried weight. Yet she had only one vote among nine Councilmen, one of whom was Spear Eagle, Les Bentarm's sightless uncle.

The shallow washes and small coulees deepened into a high-walled gully spread out from the base of Rattlesnake Ridge. Its rough sides reflected the slicing power of storm water and the scour of fierce winds.

Engle braced his feet against the floorboards as the jeep slid into the gully in a rattle of small stones and clouds of dust.

"The conglomerate mix in this cut bank could build a good-sized dam," he muttered, tilting precariously in his seat.

"It makes a pretty good road on the bottom of the gully too," Mak remarked. In a final spray of gravel from the back wheels, he righted the jeep expertly and started it along the base of the ridge. The jeep rocked over the hard incline of the bed until, at a bend in the gully, their way was entirely blocked by a scattering of boulder-sized igneous rocks. Mak changed gears in order to back out and seek a smoother passage.

"Hold it, Mak," said Engle. "We can roll most of those stones out of the way. I've got a crowbar that'll loosen them. Together we can clear them out and go on."

They pried out the hot, heavy rocks and lifted and rolled them aside. It was back-breaking work.

Suffocating downdrafts caused by rising desert heat sucked through the gully walls from off the lava slopes. Mak's heavy-soled boots took care of two scorpions that

126

scuttled away from under the loosened rocks.

Engle's persistence annoyed him. Yet his respect deep-•
ened for this fellow worker with the pink skin and narrow
back and weak eyes, who worked and sweated like a day
laborer.

Engle stooped to examine a small fragment of stone
that his iron bar brought to light from under one of the
boulders.

"What do you have there?" Mak asked, dragging his
forearm across his sweating forehead.

"Looks like a fossilized rhino's tooth." Engle spoke casually, as though rhinos were as common as jackrabbits in
Makosica. He handed the small bit to Mak.

Mak turned the lengthy, chipped object over in his
hands. "It's a fossilized tooth, all right," he agreed.

They were finding fossils at Rattlesnake Ridge after all!

He returned the tooth to the scientist and waited for
further comment. Engle grinned as he slipped it into his
pants pocket. "Guess I'll keep this one for my wa-sic."

"Wa-sic must be found in danger, Coza," Mak reminded his friend.

Engle gave him a quizzical smile. "Well, aren't we on
dangerous ground?"

Danger of rattlers and scorpions, danger of sunstroke,
yes. Danger of differences in belief, such as in the sky picture. Danger in Engle's pushing his cause before the Tribal
Council. The right time hadn't come to tell him about
that . . .

Mak glanced up the sides of the hogback that had
erupted from the center of the earth millions of years ago.
"I guess this ground was plenty dangerous, all right, when

127

that rhino hid his tooth away for your wa-sic power."

Engle spit on his hands and went to work prying out another stone. "I like the way you put it, Mak. With strong wa-sic working for both of us, we can't lose."

Moments later, true to Engle's prophecy, they made another fossil discovery.

They had cleared the way of rocks and driven to the end of the gully. Engle alighted and scrambled up the gully wall ahead of Mak, who remained behind to unload light gear from the jeep.

Reaching the rim, Engle paused to mop his face and study the mountain of lava above him. He called to Mak. "I wonder if it's safe to leave the jeep down there below the Ridge."

"Nothing around here to bother it," Mak answered, slinging the strap of Engle's binoculars over his shoulder. "I haven't seen a single rattler that wants to hide under our seat cushions."

"Okay, okay," his companion answered from above. "Anyway, I've seen so many rattlers by this time, they don't scare me anymore. I just happened to think that if it rains, run-off from this ridge could turn the gully into a raging torrent. In minutes it would bury the jeep beneath rocks and rubble."

Coza made wishful thinking about rain a worry. Even so, Mak had known flash floods in other years that turned dry washes to torrents in minutes.

"Does your rhino-power show proof that rain can fall out of a hot dry sky, Coza?"

"Hardly," his employer admitted. "Even so, I am reminded that storm water has rushed down this lava ridge

128

for ages and carved out all those coulees we've just crossed. As an earth scientist I am interested — "

Engle broke off his scientific discourse to stare at a rounded mound at his feet. He took up a small whitish chip from it and examined it closely, then picked up another to examine it, and another.

"I'm standing on the carapace of an ancient land turtle, Mak," he announced calmly. "Some poor reptile too slow to escape the end of the lava flow as it cooled."

Mak climbed the bank of the gully to take a look. Together they sorted through the small broken bits of lime-like fossil that made up the dusty shallow mound. Above them a vulture drifted curiously in the hot vault of the sky.

Mak had read about lava flows in Engle's books on the bunkhouse shelf. He studied the reddish-brown honeycomb of lava rock at his feet, then scanned the rim of the gully and its spill of loose gravel. Conglomerate, Engle called it.

He said, "Or could be this turtle was buried in ocean sediment long before the lava erupted. After the ocean receded, weathering of the sedimentary rock where it died would have brought it to the surface here."

"You have a point there," Engle conceded, pleased with Mak's scientific reasoning. "The sun hurts my eyes and I didn't examine the mound as closely as I might. Anyway, Mak, you've proved that paleontologists often differ."

At the moment another angle of their discussion was more important to Mak. "Is this an important fossil, Coza?"

"Not really, Mak. Fossilized land turtles such as this

one are fairly common in our West. However, such dis-
coveries often lead to remains of other animals that lived
at the same time in history — camels, cats, tiny horses,
rhinos — with long teeth." Engle grinned and patted the
pocket that housed his power piece. He began to salvage
bits of the ancient turtle's carapace and placed them carefully in his rock kit for further study. "The base of this
isolated igneous hogback could turn out to be a bone-
hunter's paradise after all," he said.

Engle's confidence gave Mak a lift. Excited by this
forecast, he took up the picks and shovels. Together they
began to move across the hot, barren "bone-hunter's paradise" in a search for fossils of camels, cats, tiny horses,
rhinos — with long teeth.

"What if we uncover the whole skeleton of a mastodon?
How would we ever get it out?"

"We'd rent a two-ton truck with an air drill from the
Whitehorn Garage, and dig the skeleton out piece by
piece."

Coza had an answer to everything.

For over three hours they poked around in the rock and
dust and heat at the base of Rattlesnake Ridge. They
turned up nothing to add to the bits from the land turtle's
carapace and the rhino's tooth.

Characteristically, Engle by-passed defeat. He leaned
on his pick handle, daubed sweat from his face, and
squinted up the hot, corrugated slopes of the ridge above
them.

"How far is it up there to those marks you've been telling me about, Mak?"

"Close to the top. To the right of the head of the snake."

"Weren't we planning to take a look?"

Mak felt a sickening need for haste to get away from Rattlesnake Ridge. Tell Coza about his tribesmen's demand that they appear before the Tribal Council tomorrow night. Get it over with.

He said, "We might wait for a cooler day."

There would be no cooler days, of course, unless it rained, which wasn't likely. No more time, and not much use, to look for any more fossils today.

Charles Engle gave him a gentle shove. "Lead on, Mak. We can stop on the way and eat our sandwiches in the shade of the overhang that makes up the head of the snake. We should get a whale of a view from there, too. And maybe a little breeze."

Mak started the climb.

20 View from Rattlesnake Ridge

The skin of molten lava that coated Rattlesnake Ridge millions of years before had wrinkled as it cooled, leaving a sharp corded surface. The sun-baked porous rock burned through Mak's thick-soled boots. As he climbed, small crawling creatures slid away from under his feet into dry clumps of growth anchored along the rocky ridges. He held his shovel ready, hoping that his weak-sighted friend would not see the danger.

They paused only briefly to catch breath and wipe sweat. Finally, they reached the giant rock overhang that curved upward to form the viper's head at the rim of the ridge.

Engle tossed off his hat and dropped on the rug of shade. He took a long drink from his canteen, then brought out his binoculars. "Here lies some of the wildest country known to man," he remarked quietly, sweeping his powerful lenses slowly back and forth.

Mak leaned the shovels against a wall of tilted rock, having made certain of crawlers before he seated himself.

They surveyed the panorama of the badlands stretched out at their feet while they ate the sandwiches that Gail had spread for them.

The land lay silent and forbidding, like the end of the world, uncontrolled by Man. Even without binoculars, it offered Mak dozens of landmarks. Heaps of whitened skulls of cattle that died in long-ago blizzards; small grotesque trees twisted and stunted almost out of recognition by wind and drought. Pinky's Thumb.

Aloof and majestic above a deadly sparkle of white alkali, the bent column of pink rock beckoned him. At its feet lay the low hump that had been his home, its remains already sinking into a grave of drifting sand.

Mak's breathing became a pain. He had been content at Halfway House with Pop and Mary, the truckers and tourists. He had found all his needs met in the magnificent silences of the perpendicular cliffs and white flats and level, shadow-dappled buttes. He had not been drawn into strange, threatening events that happened millions of years ago. Maybe Les Bentarm was right when he said that the best thing the whites can do for us is to stay away from us.

"What's the name of that long ridge jutting out to our right, Mak?"

"That's the front end of Big Bench," Mak said, once more the guide, giving information, and thankful that Engle's powerful glasses could detect only the top of the Bench. The dangerous canyon that circled it lay hidden by the tip of Rattlesnake Ridge.

Engle sighed. "I wish Jim would find that horse. It means so much to him. We hardly see him anymore. He's either nursing Chinook Boy or riding off at daybreak to capture the sire."

"Right." Jim wore an armor of defiance these days, giving Mak accusing stares that made him feel guilty and miserable. He missed Jim's horse talk, his speech corrections, his big-brother bossiness.

"Think that wild stallion's still over there, Mak?"

"He's got to be there because Jim has to find him." .

Engle swung his glasses to another direction. "That streak of dust across the slope ahead of us. It's moving too fast for a horsebacker. Now it's disappeared altogether — like a ghost into the earth!"

Mak studied the feather of dust. "Could be a dust-devil. Or do you think it *is* a ghost, Coza?" he asked guardedly.

Engle returned to his sandwich. "All lands have their

133

secrets and mysteries. Take a place like this — wild, brooding, unexplored. A man looking out over it could believe almost anything."

"Like what?"

Engle scanned Makosica as though leafing through the pages of a science book. "A man believing in ghosts might feel that the red-stained sheet of granite at the base of Indian Rock betrays iron, with copper and zinc not far away. Or he might believe that these vast acres of alkali flats could be a storehouse of chemicals. And if a man believed in statistics as well as in ghosts, Mak, he would consider the fact that two-thirds of America's coal beds lie under the plains and tablelands of our West, of which your Makosica is an important part."

Mak remained silent. Why tell Engle that the white man wanted to change Nature to his own way; the Indian lived in it as it was.

"Back at headquarters," Engle went on, "there's a room lined with maps and a tote board, fitted out with pumps and other gadgets, that ticks off how fast America is using up its iron and mineral fuels and water."

Mak looked straight ahead, far off and deep into his native desert homeland. "So?"

"So it's like listening to your heart beat, Mak."

After a moment Engle added, "But to get back to the present. For the last hour or so I've believed that someone's been watching us. Maybe it's only a ghost. Or my imagination."

It wasn't any of those. Mak had caught a glint of metal through that line of lifting dust. Les Bentarm, on his motorcycle, had been spying on them while they looked for fossils at Rattlesnake Ridge. Les would report to the Tribal Council tomorrow night.

To divert Engle's thoughts, Mak picked up a small bit of crystalline rock at his knee. "Sedimentary. Limestone."

"Right," Engle agreed between bites of Mrs. Barrack's homemade bread spread with peanut butter.

"And this one's shale," Mak said of another reddish-brown piece. "No," he corrected himself hastily, "shist. Because shist is finer-layered and stronger. Neither of them are igneous rock, so they don't belong on Rattlesnake Ridge. They had to be blown up here by high winds."

Engle gave his pleased smile. "You have good rock sense, Mak. You'll make a good geologist."

Mak flung the bits of rock aside. "I'd have to go to college to become a geologist. Or a paleontologist like you. I don't like school that much."

Charles Engle peeled the wrapping from the last sandwich. He offered half of it to Mak, who shook his head. "School helps us to see ourselves more clearly. Among other things, it helps us to look toward the future. But schooling doesn't hold all the answers."

Mak found himself on the defensive. "Mary Sits' nephew, Joseph Blackstone, is going to a college back East. He's learning to become some kind of an engineer. The kind that works with water."

"Great — especially if Joseph learns how to make water work for the good of thirsty land. Your people have fine minds, Mak. Many of you profit from higher learning. Others may find themselves cramped by it, same as white people."

135

There again — "know what's right and best so as you can choose for yourself."

Mak envied Joseph Blackstone for his know-how, but he felt put out with the absent young Indian for deserting the land of his people.

Engle got to his feet. He brushed bread crumbs from his lap, slapped dust from the seat of his jeans. "Now, Mak, let's have a look at those marks you found in the lava rock."

While Mak collected the gear, Engle swept his binoculars once more across Makosica.

"Looks like a scattering of long wooden crates on that rocky knoll just below us. Or am I seeing things again, Mak?"

"Those are coffins on Happy Hunting Ground Hill," Mak explained, shovels in hand. "It's the kind of place white men call a cemetery. Some of our people don't bury their dead ones. Instead, they lay them in boxes and set them high on boulders or scaffolds away from prowling animals. And closer to the Great Spirit."

Charles Engle nodded, familiar with such practices among native peoples.

Mak added as they resumed the climb, "Relatives leave things the dead ones have loved or honored, to take with them to the Spirit World — spears, gun cases, thimbles, playthings like antelope rattles. Finally their bodies go back to our Mother, the Earth."

"You say that some of your people leave their dead above the ground, Mak. Not all of you do?"

"Our older Indians hold to the old-time way, but now most of us use cemeteries for our dead — either the cemetery behind the church at the Agency, or the one near the Mission in the mountains."

"How does the Great Spirit look upon this change-over from the native way to the white man's way with the dead, Mak?"

"The Great Spirit doesn't care about change so long as we stay Indian in our hearts." Mak broke off. Was that his voice speaking?

"Well said, Mak. You have the answer to one of the biggest problems of your people today. That is, to remain Indian in your own land while learning to survive with fair standards in the white man's way. You yourself are doing very well at that."

Engle's praise overwhelmed Mak with a sense of guilt. He stayed Indian at heart all right, but he wasn't learning to survive with fair standards either as Indian *or* as white.

"Tell me, what made these marks?"

Mak pointed to the short series of worn depressions set in solid lava near the upper rim of Rattlesnake Ridge.

His wa-sic dangled on its string as he learned forward. His cowlick bristled above the shorter hair plastered to his forehead with sweat.

The bone man had turned his homeland of pink peaks and white flats upside down, seeing it in terms of slimy swamps and thrashing monsters. Then he explained away its scorched and barren Indian desert with ghosts of chemicals and coal.

He dared to defy the spirits in the sky picture with talk about thin air, hot air, cool. How would he account for these mysterious marks that seemed to come from nowhere? And went nowhere.

Engle squatted down for a closer examination of the marks in the rock. "The trowel, please, Mak."

Excitement threaded Engle's voice whenever he made a new find, no matter how unlikely. No fossils in lava, of course. Yet Mak felt a matching excitement as he watched his companion dig wind-blown soil out of the shallow depressions, then brush final particles away with a whiskbroom carried in his hip pocket.

Engle's crablike posture, his scalded face goggled in black, made him seem like some superhuman being from another world.

"You have led us to a remarkable find!" he exclaimed, leaning back on his haunches to grin up at Mak. "These depressions certainly were made by the feet of some prehistoric animal."

"What kind of animal?" All at once Mak could believe almost anything of this incredible science-man. That Coza might hold a white-man power in his rhino's tooth, strong enough to translate the eroded footprints into a prehistoric beast able to defy molten lava. And leave its bones to be dug out centuries later ...

"We'll never know what kind of animal," Engle answered practically. He measured the imprints, chipped bits of lava to store in his kit for later study. "The remains of the animal that waded to his death here are lost in history, Mak. Incinerated to ashes."

Mak blurted, "I knew that all the time. From the books."

He felt as though an end had come.

Here was the time to deliver Cloud Rise's message.

138

Mak said harshly, looking down at Engle's narrow shoulders, "The Tribal Council wants to talk to you about your right to dig on Indian land. It meets tomorrow night in the Dogtown Council Lodge below the Agency on the river. Mary Sits sent word by Cloud Rise for us to be there."

"I expected that sooner or later," Engle answered, chipping away without looking up. "They want me to get off their land before I have a chance to discover something of importance here," he added, somewhat testily. "Is that why they sent Les Bentarm scouting after us on his motorcycle?"

So Engle knew it was Les after all, not a ghost.

Mak made a lame reply. "Les rides all over the reservation. Could be he was out here poking around on his own."

Charles Engle closed his rock kit and got to his feet. "Does Les sit on the Tribal Council, Mak?"

"Les sits there to help his uncle, Spear Eagle, who is sick and blind. Mary Sits is on the Council, too," Mak added as a note of encouragement.

"Be good to see Mary again." Engle laid his arm over Mak's bare shoulders. He stared across the alkali flats that sparkled like beds of diamonds at the base of Rattlesnake Ridge. "Okay, Mak. We'll do our best to make a case for ourselves out of what we've already discovered." He added in friendly partnership, "I'm sure our presentation will bring the Council around to our way of thinking."

Our presentation . . . Bring the Council to *our* way of thinking.

What did Coza mean? If Coza thought for a minute that he would side —

Mak checked an angry retort, brushed Engle's words aside. Coza's belief that the Council would accept his handful of fossils and grant his permit was an empty belief. Like Coza's talk about wealth in Makosica, it would come to nothing.

Yet, this white man knew about many things in Nature that the Indian people — Earth People — never heard of. He was certain in his beliefs, able to prove them. Such as the evolving of fossils from bones of ancient animals; the logic of mirages caused by air.

Charles Engle continued to look out over Makosica, his arm across Mak's shoulders. Not holding him. Just there. Looking.

Mak stood beside him, looking to Makosica, too. Looking for answers.

The silence between them was broken by a faint monotonous rattling sound that came from the rocks behind them. It grew steadily louder. Finally its ominous meaning cut through Mak's thoughts.

He wheeled about to stare into the eyes of a rattlesnake coiling in readiness to strike at the calf of Charles Engle's leg.

"Watch it!" Mak gave Engle a shove forward.

The hammer flew from Engle's hand as he lurched clear of the snake. Mak reached for his shovel. With a single jab he drove the edge of it into the middle of the springing coil. The next moment the reptile's mangled form was squirming helplessly at their feet.

Engle jerked off his hat to wipe sweat that ran down his forehead. "I guess a man never sees so many rattlers that he's not scared of them. That snake was about to set its poisonous fangs into my leg. Thanks to you, Mak, it didn't make it."

"We could have got down the ridge in time, to your snakebite kit in the jeep," Mak muttered shakily.

"No, Mak, we couldn't have. You see, I left my snakebite kit back home, in the bunkhouse. Too far away to be of any help."

They gazed at one another, realizing their close brush with death.

What could you do about a man so smart and so foolishly forgetful, Mak wondered? To forget like that proved Coza needed help in his smartness.

Help against the dangers of Makosica. Help before the astute Indian councilmen when he explained his smattering of weird objects.

Mak thought, "I'll have to stand by him tomorrow night or he won't make it."

He lifted his canteen and drank in long gulps until it was empty.

Engle stepped carefully around the dead snake and retrieved his hammer. He gave a final glance at the footprints in the rock that angled off to nowhere. "We've had us quite a view from the Ridge today, haven't we, Mak?"

Mak nodded. Quite a view of Makosica, a view of Engle. And of himself.

"You lead the way down, Mak," Engle added with a grin. "I feel a little queasy. Must be the heat."

21 Council Meeting at Dogtown

The Dogtown Council Lodge below the Indian Agency had the same mud-chinked, octagonal log walls and dirt roof as in the days when Mary first brought him there. It was surrounded by the same Indian haylands, and flanked by the same village of prairie-dog mounds from which it got its name.

Mary's eyes met his when he came through the blanket-hung doorway with Engle. She sat at the Council table, and turned at once to give attention to one of the speakers, for the meeting already had started with unfinished business.

Mak studied her strong aboriginal profile silhouetted against the wall. What did Mary's power hold for Coza and himself tonight?

No matter what might be ruled against him later, it was good to sink hastily to the plank floor near the entrance, beside his pals and classmates. Pete Light Thunder, Moses Painter, and bulky Joe Whip, breathless from hurrying ahead of his parents to sit with the other boys.

Out of respect for their elders seated before the Council table and lined against the log walls, the boys grinned a silent greeting to Mak, pommeled his shoulder, and made brief, jerky hand-talk.

Charles Engle refused a folding chair in the center audience of hay farmers and cattle ranchers, the Agency laborers and their families. Instead, he dropped his lanky frame to the floor beside Mak and the boys. His pink, peeling face and sunbleached hair stood out in the dark-skinned assembly like an albino in a buffalo herd.

Valley farmers in loose work shirts and jeans had opened the meeting with complaint to Council Chief Painter against white farmers across the river from the reservation.

"They keep taking more than their rights to the irrigation water," Longhorn was saying.

"That leaves our reservation ditches empty with only mud," Racer reported. "Our crops burn up in the drought."

"So we don't get no hay money to buy grub for our kids this winter." Light Thunder, Pete's father, lifted a brown fist in emphasis.

Painter, handsome in a new yellow shirt and fresh haircut, turned to a young stranger standing with other young Indians along the log wall.

"Mr. Emil Berry here, new Agency clerk," Painter informed the assembled Indians. "He takes the civil service exam from Osage in Oklahoma. Then the government sends him here. Tonight he speaks for Superintendent Stoner, who is away. So, Berry, you tell us why we don't get our fair share of river water."

The young clerk from the southern tribe looked up from a note pad on his bent knee. Mak noted hazel eyes, much like his own, and a tanned face.

"Superintendent Stoner has ordered our ditch riders to double-check the white farmer's sluice gates," Berry told

them. "When he returns, Mr. Stoner will name a committee from among your Councilmen to take your case before
the County's Irrigation Council that sits in Whitehorn next
month."

Berry spoke slowly so that Tall Man, the uniformed
Agency police officer, could interpret his words to the old
fullbloods seated on the floor between the hay farmers and
the Council table. Two Moons, their aging medicine man;
Bird Rattle, his wrinkled face streaked with ashes in
mourning for his dead wife; Crawler, fingering the signal
mirror on his chest; the touseled-headed Sweetgrass; the
bespectacled Cloud Rise, whose wa-sic was powerless to
recover his lost horse against the fearful Spirit Face.

Mak found an inner strength in the huddled dignity of
these elders. And in the scent of woodsmoke and tanned
buckskin that came from their graying braids and frayed
moccasins as they listened from their traditional position
close to the earth.

Following Tall Man's interpretation, Blackbird countered quickly at his place beside Painter. "Stoner's already
made irrigation committees to speak for us, Berry. Then he
goes off somewheres with nothing done to back us up."

The disgruntled murmur from the audience left no need
for interpretation, even among the fullbloods.

Emil Berry might be new to the northern reservation,
but he was informed on the irrigation situation of its people. "You've had little or no runoff from rain or snow for
three years," he reminded them. "Every farmer in this
river valley, Indian or white, is low on irrigation water
during drought. Even with whites taking only their share,
you Indian farmers will be short in dry years. That is, until

a higher dam is built on the river to hold back more of the spring snowmelt from your mountains."

At mention of a higher dam, a young Indian in a red windband leaned forward quickly from the shadows of the wall to stare at Emil Berry.

"Who is that man?" Engle asked at Mak's shoulder.

Mak shook his head, angered with himself for failing to recognize one of his own people.

Bird Rattle jerked up his blackened face as though wakened from a deep sleep. "Why don't the White Father in Washington build us a higher dam then?" he inquired in sign.

Defeated in his fight to save his buffalo and his homeland, Bird Rattle now existed on rations issued from the Agency commissary. He held to the childish belief that a distant beneficent White Father, who granted salt pork and tea and crackers, also granted dams.

"The United States government will supply funds to help build us a new dam," Emil Berry answered, "but we Indians must furnish the material and labor."

The old signal mirror glistened on Crawler's chest as he replied from his position on the floor. "We are not like the beaver who can build a dam of sticks and mud."

"It's always the same thing." Flanked by his nephew Les Bentarm in helmet and war paint, the sightless Spear Eagle complained from the end of the council table. "Whites get money and cement for their dams. They get water to save their crops. And if a new dam ever is built, they get the jobs, too."

Mak had a feeling that Spear Eagle had been briefed by his nephew on the hopelessness of jobs for Indians. Les knew through bitter experience.

"Yeah." Joe Braids and two companions backed up Spear Eagle. They lolled against the log wall behind the old Indian and Les. Like a bodyguard, Mak thought.

"When a higher dam is built," Emil Berry said, "all able-bodied Indians will get the work — if they want to work. And if they take the trouble to learn the know-how."

The clerk touched a sore spot in Les Bentarm, who wasted his time racing his motorcycle around the reservation.

Les brought his tilted chair down beside his uncle with an angry thud. "We've waited years on a dam. We want action. Now. We want our share of irrigation water for crops. Now. We want work. Now."

"Yeah!" chorused his pals against the wall.

"Then get ready for it now," Berry answered them evenly. "Go into government training programs. Learn how to become truck mechanics, draftsmen, cooks for work crews."

Les reddened beneath his paint-streaked face. "That's right, Berry, put us off!" he shouted.

The quarrel was getting out of hand. Painter hastened to shelve the argument over water rights for another meeting, and went into the main order of business.

He called Dr. Charles Engle to stand before the Council.

"Engle, we hear that you have come to dig something out of Makosica. This is our land and you must have our consent to do that. We called you here to show us what you plan to take out of our Makosica and why. If we will let you."

Les Bentarm, of course, was Painter's informant. While Engle was waiting for car repair in Whitehorn, Les had listened to his initial inquiry regarding a permit, and later spied on him at Rattlesnake Ridge.

Charles Engle nodded brief recognition of the stony, painted Les. He accepted the challenge in Painter's tone. As though relieved that the wrangle over water rights was ended, he hurried to empty the contents of his rock kit before Painter and the Councilmen, then began his plea for a permit to excavate. He was courteous, confident, almost cocky. The way he looked when he held a trump card at poker with Jim Barrack, Mak thought a little uneasily.

His heart ached for Coza. Coza knew so much about fossils, had so pitifully few to show.

Engle introduced himself to the assembly of Indians as a paleontologist, sent from their state college to search for fossilized bones. Bones of ancient animals that lived in Makosica millions of years ago, when oceans and swampland covered much of the earth. He indicated his small heap of bones as proof of their existence in Makosica.

During those centuries, Engle went on, eruptions from deep inside the earth changed the oceans and swamps to rock and soil and forests, and brought the buried bones to light. Among the ancient animals that lived on Indian homeland was the massive triceratops, one of the largest creatures ever to walk the face of the earth.

Crawler's cry of outraged disbelief interrupted Tall Man's blundering interpretation of Engle's words.

"I can't understand the big words," Tall Man told his Council Chief. "I can't give them back the right way to our people."

147

"Who can tell what this white man is talking about?" Looking as helpless as Tall Man, Painter's eyes focused on Councilman Wings. Withdrawn and wooden as a pagan priest in his black hat and black shawl, Wings sat at the council table beside Mary Sits.

Years ago, Wings had attended an eastern college, thinking to help his people into new ways upon his return. They were not ready to change. Scorned and ignored by them for his white man's learning, Wings went back to the blanket. No one ever heard him speak English again.

Painter turned from the closed face and deaf ears of Wings to appeal to Emil Berry, the new Agency clerk.

Berry shook his head. He had trained to become a clerk, not a paleontologist.

The Council Chief read withdrawal and suspicion in the faces of his audience. He turned apologetically to Charles Engle. "Many of us have gone to our government Boarding School, but none of us can put your kind of words back into our language. If we can't understand you, Bone Man, your words are like wind in the treetops, meaning nothing. You might as well take your little pile of bones and go home."

Even though he had expected this, Painter's words of dismissal struck Mak's ears like a physical blow. Engle leave, unheard? That meant — Mak wouldn't think what it meant.

He leaped to his feet. He said to Painter, his face a mask of calm, "I know what this white man is talking about. I am his guide. I can interpret for him."

He felt Pete Light Thunder yanking at his jeans to hold him back; he shook off Engle's low-spoken warning, "Skip

148

it, Mak. Let's get out of here."

He ignored Mary Sits, matron of the tribe, unmoved as a rock in the rapids of a river.

. . . an Indian fights out his own problems . . . Even to staking himself out on the plains to fight in that spot until he dies . . .

The dark faces of his fellow tribesmen swam before him. Before he could begin the interpretation, Mak sensed their minds resisting.

He listened now, as Engle resumed his talk, then, at the first pause, broke into the simple rhythm of the tongue Mary had taught him.

He joined the learned earth scientist to bring out a new legend of change in Makosica.

Mak knew the story by heart. He defined the long words related to the great prehistoric animals — paleontologist, diastrophic, dinosaurs — "big as our Agency barn." He enlarged on Engle's description — "with thrashing tails and little heads. But when the swamps dried up, bone men say the dinosaurs died out. Their big bodies and small brains couldn't change to a different life when the earth changed."

As though proceeding with a careful plan, Engle went on to explain that ages of earth pressure had turned the animals' buried bones into stone, called fossils.

"In that way," Mak added, again overstepping his role as interpreter, "our Earth Mother made sure that their bones would not rot away and be lost forever. Weather-wear, the earth itself always in change, brought them to view. Highway workmen helped with their shovels — "

He interpreted Engle's description of ancient animal

149

existence as the earth scientist lifted each fossil from his small harvest on the Council table. The etching of the sea creature, called mollusk, on the face of a rock found in a road cut; the pieces of petrified wood; the crumbling chip of the land turtle's carapace, and the battered rhino's tooth — which Engle now wore as his wa-sic — both found at Rattlesnake Ridge.

Finally he interpreted Engle's account of the ancient animal footprints in hardened lava that Mak himself discovered on the upper slope.

Here was visible evidence, Engle told the wooden-faced listeners, that entire skeletons of prehistoric animals must lie beneath their Makosica. He requested a permit from the Council to locate and excavate them. He would take nothing more. He would not harm their sacred land.

Engle stepped back from the Council table and awaited their decision.

The stunned silence in the log lodge roared in Mak's ears, broken only by the yap of a prairie dog from the mounds outside.

Maybe, if they knew why — caught in the web of his own belief, Mak took it upon himself to explain why.

"There is good reason to dig out these skeletons. They will be wired together and set up for people to see how the animals looked. When we learn about the old-time animals of Makosica, and other things that lived on earth before us, we learn about ourselves. How we got here. How to understand one another — "

He broke off. The Indian and the white man understand one another?

How had his wa-sic led him to hint of such an understanding before this august assemblage of his people? Especially tonight, when drought had their backs to the wall, and they were deprived and angered by a century of misunderstanding with white men that continued even into present-day denial of their water rights.

The silence that followed his plea filled the Council Lodge like that between lightning flash and thunder clap.

22 Message of Makosica

Crawler was first to find voice. He ignored Mak, to address Engle coldly, while he fingered the signal mirror on his chest.

"The white man always thinks he knows more than the Indian. By our legends we know that Makosica was made by spirits to drive off our enemies. It was not made by a power deep inside the earth. Indian legend tells no silly stone-bone stories about oceans and swamps in Makosica where giant monsters thrashed about. Before the spirits changed Makosica, it was a dry grassland with our own hoofed animals grazing there. That is all."

"Let dead things lie in Makosica where they fall," said the tangle-headed Sweetgrass. "It is bad medicine to move their bones. Spirit Face will be angry and punish us."

Sweetgrass returned to staring at his Mother, the Earth, through the cracks in the floor.

Two Moons signaled to speak from his cross-legged position. The other Indians contained their rising anger against Engle and Mak, to wait in respectful silence while their medicine man addressed them. He was interpreter for the spirits. His ceremonies had worked. They had heard his long discourses on the abuses of white men at every Council meeting. How they must keep their Mother, the Earth, whole in order to survive. That land was their religion, the measure of all life. Already the whites had scarred it with plows and roads and mines and holes for fence posts that divided the land for a few, when it was meant for all.

"We must not let this white man with his crazy story dig into our Makosica," Two Moons shouted to Painter in closing.

A rising growl of distrust of the white man swept through the Council Lodge.

Wasta wanitch! Not good. Bad ... bad ... the old Indians refused to break with tradition, proof or not.

The hay farmers and Agency laborers moved uneasily in their folding chairs and along the wall. They had attended school. They read newspapers. But their unformed opinions were swayed by their legendary upbringing and by the aroused distrust of their elders. Longhorn's baby cried out in its sleep. The worried mother hastened to cover its mouth with her hand.

Joe Whip, Sr., addressed Mak from his seat among them. "We don't need to look at no animal skeletons built

152

from stone-bones to understand white people. Our empty bellies do that for us."

Embittered by the change in his nephew since his return from the city, Spear Eagle's sightless rage struck out at all white men through Charles Engle. "You whites are twisting the minds of our youth," he declared from his seat at the Council table. "Now you make our Makosica Mike speak with a forked tongue against his own land, his own people. You have done this to him, Bone Man, so that he will help you take what you want out of Makosica."

Mak began to shake before Spear Eagle's accusation. Wronged they were by many white men, but not by this white man.

"That's not so, Spear Eagle," he answered. "This white man has not made me speak against Makosica. He has made me speak for it. He has brought me to know it differently and to hold to it even closer than ever before."

The venerable Councilman drew his scrap of blanket about him, outraged at Mak's disrespectful denial. "Tell this dangerous white man to go back to his college, Painter. Before he destroys both our land and our youth!"

The force of Spear Eagle's emotion sent him into a fit of coughing.

Les Bentarm sprang to his feet beside the shaking shoulders of the overwrought old Indian. His uncle's anger split open all his own stored-up rancor. Mak caught the full force of it in the brittle glare of his dark eyes.

"We don't want to hear nothing more out of you, Malloy, or out of your white boss-man, either," he told Mak hoarsely. "You were born of an Irish trucker. You were raised white and you put in with a white rancher to stay white. Now you follow after a white man to dig made-up things out of our sacred land. Your divided blood forks your tongue with lies to speak his fancy words."

Les turned to address their Council Chief. "He is traitor and no part of us, Painter. I say, send him away with the white man. I *throw* him away!"

Les Bentarm lifted his right fist high. He swung it downward past his side, then opened his hand. He gave Makosica Mike Malloy the sign of the closed hand. Threw him away into the shadows behind him, along with the despised white man.

A trembling set itself up inside Mak. The thing he feared most had come.

Strip him of his inheritance. Cast him off from the tribe. Another Wings who walked the land of his people but was no longer a part of them. Banishment from Makosica meant death to him as an Indian. Better to go to Pop in California . . .

No wa-sic was strong enough to help him now.

Mak felt Engle's hand on his shoulder to steady his trembling.

"Before you pass judgment on Mak, Painter," Engle said, "may I have another word?"

At Painter's nod, once again Engle addressed the assembled Indians. He spoke as though all he had said before led to this final word.

"You will not break with your tradition," he began quietly. "You will not believe that oceans and upheavals and giant animals once existed in your Makosica. Even when your eyes see proof. Even when one of your own sons tells you the truth about it. Will you believe, then, that because it has undergone centuries of earth changes, Makosica has become a land filled with great wealth, far more important than any fossils I ever can hope to dig out of it?"

Along with the others, Mak stared at Charles Engle. Was this more of Coza's visionary babbling about the wonders of Makosica?

Engle's storybook words brought the stormy Les Bent-arm to his feet. "What do you mean, white man? You'd better be right when you say a thing like that to us. Forget how Makosica was made — by spirits or by floods and earthquakes with crazy animals mixed up in it. Whatever. We *know* there's nothing there now. Except dust and rock and rattlesnakes and tumbleweeds. We're not in a mood to be fooled anymore by you."

Les drew out his knife and dropped it with a clatter on the Council table. "You'd better tell it straight, white man," he warned.

Charles Engle ignored the knife as though his eyes were too weak to see it. "While searching for fossils, I came to know your Makosica," he continued as though he had not been interrupted. "I have caught its message, which is that of survival through change. You are a fortunate people because you are made from the rich stuff of your land. Your minds, your bodies, your gods are a part of the constant effort of your Earth Mother to survive against great odds of change."

Engle paused for Tall Man to catch up with his interpretation, then continued.

"I tell you straight, when I say there is enough wealth in

Makosica to feed your children for many winters to come, to furnish you with modern homes and cars and electric washing machines. And above all, with more than enough river water for irrigation. So, will you believe," he demanded of his astonished listeners, "that you have enough sand in Makosica to make all the cement you need to build half a dozen dams on your river to save your crops? Will you believe you have thousands of tons of alkali, or gypsum powder, to harden the cement, with enough left over to stock a plant with fertilizer to cover all the hayfields in Montana? And that there may be tungsten to market for hardening metal — granite, iron, copper, zinc? Not to forget coal left in mines by early prospectors to generate power to make electricity. Will you believe that all this waits before your eyes in your own desertland," Engle demanded, "if only you will train your eyes to *see?*"

Engle struck his fist on the Council table to emphasize his last words. He stared back at them through his thick glasses.

They stirred uneasily, like a kettle trembling before it breaks into a boil.

For a moment the lift in Mak's heart pushed aside his pain and humiliation as an outcast.

Good for Coza! He knew more of Indian nature and the real value of Makosica than he himself ever dreamed. When the issue of water rights came up, Coza had listened and tied it in with his knowledge of the rock and mineral value of Makosica for building their dam. He held to that thought until the right moment. It was his trump card. And he played it now.

The young Indian in the red windband lifted his arm

for permission to speak.

Ting! Like that, Mak recognized him as Joseph Blackstone, Mary Sits' nephew.

Joseph had come back from college!

"This white man speaks with a straight tongue, Painter," Joseph said. "We *can* build us a dam out of the sand and gravel and minerals of Makosica. When I was a boy, wandering all over Makosica, my Dream came. It told me that the spirits, in their cunning, had hidden a mysterious wealth beneath the plainsland they destroyed."

He had kept his Dream secret, Joseph said, fearing he would not be understood when he left the reservation to try to find the answer. He worked his way through college and studied as a hydraulic engineer. Now he was back, Joseph concluded, with the way to help his people make that Dream come true.

Mak watched as Joseph stood shaking hands with Charles Engle. The Dream in the eyes of the Indian and the white man matched and held. They began talking business about it.

The Osage clerk, Emil Berry, hurried forward, followed by other young men from along the wall. The hay farmers pushed back their chairs to join into a tight group. They interrupted the heated meeting with talk about gravel trucks, Geiger counters, cement mixers, drag lines, pay checks. Mak heard Emil Berry say he would urge Superintendent Stoner to get working on it right away. "In another year, our wa-sic will back up our hopes for a new dam . . ."

Someone let out a war whoop. Mort Minnow, the tribe's musician, beat on the drum in the corner.

The old Indians on the floor began to scold at the wild

157

confusion, the talk they could not understand.

Painter blew his eagle-bone whistle for quiet.

Mary Sits, tribal matron, rose to weave a thread of order through the hubbub. She spoke in the dignity of her mother tongue, and accompanied her native words with hand-signs, pausing for Tall Man's interpretation.

"We are Earth People. Our earth is sacred. But we have thrashed about on our desertland like those great animals with brains too small to understand the good it holds. It takes a white man to prove to us that oceans and quaking earth and strange animals have changed its sacredness for our own good. If our Mother, the Earth, can change, so can we."

Mary paused, realizing she moved on dangerous ground, even for a tribal matron. "My great-grandfather, Chief Earth Boy, knew we must change when he held his warriors off the wagon trains. Wings knew it. Now Joseph. Others knew and tried. Often it is hard to change. It takes time."

At the opposite end of the council table, Les Bentarm averted his eyes.

Then Mary addressed their old ones grouped at her feet. Denied their ancient way of life, it was too late for them to learn another. Native words came in gushes of stress as Mary sought to soften the blows of change for them.

"While we change our way of life, we still can keep ourselves Indian at heart, just as our changing Earth Mother still remains our mother at heart. Our oneness with the land makes this so. The scars from the gravel pits we dig to help us survive will be healed by wind and rain. So, too, will be the harmless holes dug to find old bones."

Mary turned to the Council Chief. Only her pained dark eyes showed how it hurt to override the wishes of her elders. "Painter, I say give our good friend, the Bone Man, his piece of paper. Let him dig for his fossils wherever they lie in Makosica."

Mak watched while all eyes fastened upon the slim, pink-skinned white man, whose weak eyes had read the message of survival in their Makosica. His Dream and powerful wa-sic — also of their land — had turned his message into good for all.

Painter lifted his right hand. *"Hoh."* Yes.

"Hoh ... Hoh ..." The Councilmen voted to grant Engle his permit. All except Les Bentarm, although Mak noted that Les had put his knife away. As Mary had said, it took time to change.

"Hoh ... Hoh ..." echoed the audience of Indians, spilling out their excitement over an undefined change in thought.

"Wasta," Engle said, and lifted his open hand in thanks.

Mary's power had worked for the white man. Could it work for an accused outcast?

Mak's throat tightened as Mary searched the faces of the younger Indians, restless to leap into action, yet ranged once more along the wall in respectful attention — her nephew Joseph Blackstone, Emil Berry, sons of hay farmers and cattle ranchers and laborers, his wide-eyed classmates on the floor near the entrance. Finally her glance settled on Mak, apart from the others before Painter, not knowing where else he belonged.

159

"Other young men like Chief Earth Boy rise from among us to speak and act," Mary said. "This is because their Dreams come with strong wa-sic to bring together in themselves all the powers of their people. Painter, we cannot let even one such young man go away from us now."

Painter followed Mary's glance toward Mak. It held there a long moment.

Mak waited, scarcely breathing.

Then the Council Chief gave judgment. He lifted his right arm. *"Hoh!"*

"Hoh! ... Hoh! ..."

Acquitted of disloyalty to his tribe, Makosica Mike Malloy would remain in his homeland.

Mak met Mary's eyes, and wordless gratitude to her poured out of him. Yet the ordeal of change, which he could accept for the good of his tribesmen, still fought in his own divided blood. He could not guide Engle to Spirit Face for the fossils. He was bound by traditional fear.

Mary knew the turmoil that raged within him. Her final words included all the young Indians present, but Mak knew she meant them especially for him. "The Earth is your Mother. All you ever will need to make your way can be found in her."

"Hoh!" said Painter.

The Dogtown Council Meeting was over.

23 No Time for Wind in the Treetops

It was late evening when Mak Malloy and Charles Engle returned from the Dogtown Council Meeting on the river.

The glare of moonlight whitened the ridgepole of the ranchhouse beside the cottonwood. The deserted cattle sheds and depleted haystacks adjoining the corrals held an eerie, daylight pall.

Little had been said between them during the ride across the reservation. Engle napped with his chin on his chest. Or was that a front, Mak wondered, to avoid talk?

They had stood together as brothers before the Indian Council. He had risked banishment from his tribe — defended his white friend's right to speak about the buried bones of Makosica, and about a new way of life for Indian people in their own land.

In so doing, Coza turned the tide against Mak's banishment, and by-passed, as well, his shamefully delayed fossil search.

A more closely knit partnership hardly could be found between friends. Yet Mak felt a sickening sense of separation.

Fossils had been shown and accepted, the permit to dig them won. But the *important* fossil beds still remained hidden and unknown to all but himself.

Engle alighted from the jeep and hurried into the

bunkhouse. Mak remained beside the jeep. He kicked at the tires as though to test them out for tomorrow's trip. Wherever that was to be.

Engle reappeared in the bunkhouse doorway. Hastily he tore open one of the long envelopes he often received from his Foundation. He held the letter close, and strained his eyes to read in the moonlight.

Glancing up, he caught Mak watching him from beside the jeep. He grinned faintly and stuffed the letter inside his pocket as of no consequence.

Too late to hide it, Coza. The Foundation considered the badlands fossil project a failure. The Foundation had called its paleontologist back to his college.

Jim Barrack came toward them just then from the direction of the corrals. Nothing unusual in that, either. Jim prowled around the barns at all hours. Until everyone else was in bed. That way he didn't have to admit to anyone that the wild mustang on Big Bench — whether dead or alive — had got the best of him.

Jim answered their unasked question indifferently. "Loosa got a stone in her foot. I came back early to take it out." He looked from one to the other. "Get the permit?"

"Sure thing." Engle answered cheerfully from the bunkhouse doorway, as though securing the permit had been the simplest thing in the world.

"You're shot in the head with luck," Jim said with dry envy. "How about we celebrate your big win with coffee and peanut butter sandwiches?"

Jim went on toward the house and Engle fell in with him.

Mak stared after them. He never felt quite certain

whether or not Jim meant to include him in these little get-togethers. Anyway, tonight he felt relieved to avoid this one.

Across the way Gail Barrack came out of the barn door. She walked toward the corral gate, carrying an electric lantern and a pail of damp blood-stained cloths.

Mak stepped forward to open the gate for her. He was shaken over the ordeal at the Council meeting, the arrival of the letter from the Foundation. Gail's presence at the barn at this late hour spelled another disaster.

"You've brought Paint home from Reeser's pasture," he said when she stopped at the open gate.

She nodded, looking forlorn and weary, hooded by her long hair, carrying her pail of bloody cloths.

Behind them came the familiar sound of teeth grinding hay, the scent of leather and horsehair, Chinook Boy's hoarse whinny for attention.

Above the comforting sounds and smells, angry frustration at Gail's triumph rose in Mak like a heavy cloud.

"The wind changed," she explained hastily before he could speak, "and I caught Paint's whinny on it. Another duststorm's brewing. Anyway, I knew by Paint's voice that something was wrong. Jim had the stone out of Loosa's hoof, so I rode her over. Reeser's spring has gone dry. Paint and Nite Boy were frantic with thirst. They tried to break through the barbed-wire fence. Paint cut his leg. I've doctored it. He'll be okay to ride tomorrow."

"I should have checked that spring," Mak said, guilt and anger in his voice.

"It's never gone dry before. Not ever. They raced all the way back to our water tank." She skirted the real issue

163

disjointedly, as though seeking to excuse herself for defying his plan.

Mak brought it out in the open. When she started past him through the gate, he gripped the top of the low gate post so that his extended arm barred her way.

"That turkey feather headdress of Walking Crane's is no good."

"But it's all there is."

"Engle got his permit."

His words brought a flash of brightness to her face. Then hopelessness set in again. She couldn't believe that the permit made any difference. He was Indian but she knew him better than he thought. His words were only wind in the treetops. They stated a fact. Nothing more.

All at once she dropped the pail and began to pound his forearm with her fists. She wasn't blaming him. He was only part of one of her brother's wild schemes to defeat the drought and secure his future as horse rancher. She had to strike out someway. Against the hurt of having to part with Paint. Her father losing his job. The wells going dry. The chickens dying in the heat. The hope of housing a paying fossil expedition lost with the arrival of Engle's letter . . .

"Why doesn't it rain?" she choked. "Why? That isn't much to ask — just little drops of water from the sky. They could save us, those little drops — "

She lowered her head against his arm so he couldn't see her tears. And that hurt him worse than her fists.

As if ashamed of her weakness, she ducked under his arm and ran sobbing toward the house.

Mak stood gripping the top of the gatepost. He stared at the pail spilling out the damp cloths she had used to bathe wire cuts, so that Paint would be fit to trade tomorrow . . .

Why did Mary have to build him up as a second Earth Boy when she knew he was so divided and afraid? Earth Boy had much to contend with in lost homelands, wars, and starved tribesmen, but he never had contended with a divided blood.

The opposing hands came at him again, as on that morning when he searched for Shungatoga on Big Bench. Pushing, pulling, tearing him one way then the other — from sacred gods to facts on printed pages. From superstition in sky pictures to proven laws of Nature, from Irish father to Indian mother.

By now Coza was snoring gently in his bunk. One by one lights went on in the upper story of the ranchhouse, then went out again.

The lantern light still showed above the long table under the cottonwood. Jim was left alone over there.

"He's waiting me out," Mak thought bitterly. "So let him wait."

Mak took the peanut butter sandwich Gail had left for him, oozing his favorite chokecherry jelly, the way he liked it. He seated himself on the cottonwood stump beyond the light of the lantern that hung above the table.

Jim leaned across the table beside his empty coffee mug. His position put his eyes on a level with Mak's eyes.

"You missed out on the family conclave."

Mak bit into his sandwich. From here on it would be straight talk. No time now for wind in the treetops. The fact that he could depend on Jim Barrack for that, bitter as it might be, bolstered him a little.

165

"I waited up to brief you in," Jim said. "I guess Gail told you that Dad lost his job."

"She told me."

Jim went down the list. "Chuck got his orders from the Foundation to abandon his search for fossils. Know that, too?"

Mak nodded.

Jim poured coffee into a mug and pushed it along the table in Mak's direction. Waiting on me like a baby brother, Mak thought, before he chews me out.

"Chuck's got until the first of the week, though," Jim added.

Mak nodded again. He always had another chance, it seemed.

Jim ran his fingers through his hair, and let out a deep breath.

"Gail's got a notion that she must sell her beadwork collection to save the old home — like one of the corny heroines in her paperbacks. But then you knew that when you left both ponies out of her reach in Reeser's pasture. You don't want her to trade Paint for that moth-eaten headdress, either. We tried to talk her out of it tonight, too — Dad, Mom, Chuck. I made her cry."

"So did I," Mak said.

Jim looked straight at him. "I guess you know that you and I are not about to let her make this sacrifice. Not when we've got a way to stop her."

Mak nodded, like a wound-up mechancial toy. He couldn't seem to get any words out of his throat.

Jim got to his feet, yawned, and stretched his arms above his head, making double fists. Looking up, he saw a

166

dead limb of cottonwood and struck at it. The loud crash startled a bird to scolding in the upper branches.

Jim shook off a drip of blood. "Time I turned in. I'm off for Big Bench at daybreak. I happen to believe that horse is over there. The same way you believe those fossils are there. Wherever 'there' is. I don't aim to come back this time until I get what I'm after. How about you, Mak?"

Their eyes held in a kind of fixation. Neither could draw away, even if he wanted. An icy stillness filled Mak.

"Same here." His voice sounded muffled, far away. Like a stranger's.

"Turn out the light when you finish your coffee, pard."

Jim's voice trailed into a husky whisper over his shoulder as he disappeared into the house.

That last word and the way Jim said it bound them together, brothers in failure, in a final effort to stop the girl.

24 The Forgotten Whiskbroom

The early morning haze that usually veiled Makosica had taken on a smoky tinge. The murk was just heavy enough to edge the sun with a furry cast, without diminishing its heat.

At the jeep Engle said, "Looks like a storm cloud over

the badlands. Could that mean we throw in our rain gear, Mak?"

"It's only a cloud of dust. A windstorm's building." Gail Barrack answered for Mak from the back step.

Her eyes were hollow from lost sleep, following the family discussion the night before. Nothing more had been said at breakfast about her determination to ride Paint to Redrock's place to make the trade for Walking Crane's headdress. Nothing said about Engle's letter from the Foundation, or about the Tribal Council meeting. Her parents hadn't shown up for the morning meal. Mak guessed everyone knew the time for talk was over.

Engle grinned over his shoulder as he stepped into the jeep. "Even so, Gail, my rhino's tooth has gnawed at me all night to give me a sign."

"About what?" Mak slammed the end gate shut.

"Could be to remind me about how duststorms often are followed by rainstorms in order to clear the air," Engle answered.

A rainstorm would clear the air of a lot of things besides dust, thought Mak.

At the sound of the engine starting up, Mr. Barrack stepped to the kitchen door beside Gail, to scan the sky, as usual, for rain, and to wave them off.

Minutes later, when he turned the jeep off the ranch road into a shallow draw, Mak glanced back. The dark blur of father and daughter still remained at the back step.

The jeep jolted over scattered rocks and cacti in the bed of the draw, then shot out onto the sandy floor of the badlands. The time had come to level with Charles Engle.

"We're headed for one of those canyons below the base

168

of Big Bench," Mak announced. "To a place called Spirit Face."

"Sounds interesting."

"It's where I found my wa-sic," Mak went on. "Also where my Dream says the fossil beds lie. Like I told Jim, it's a dangerous place." Let Engle know again what they were in for. "That's mostly why I haven't told you. Or taken you there. The danger."

"Maybe *that's* why my wa-sic was at me all night. Not because a rainstorm's headed our way. But to warn me of danger."

"That's mostly why I didn't tell Painter, either. Anyway, you headed me off," Mak accused childishly.

Agreeably his companion shouldered the blame. "Sorry. I had a lead on a dam for the Indian hay farmers. That seemed more important just then, than to hear about a place where fossils lie buried."

Mak squirmed over the steering wheel. He wished Coza could get away from wa-sic and the dam, and face the issue between them. Stop denying his own urgent need to find fossils. Stop stringing Mak along to cover up his disappointment in an untrustworthy guide. Mak's battered Indianness cried out for anger or blame — anything to hide the frightening fact that all answers pointed to one grim destination.

"This is as far as we can drive. We'll have to walk the rest of the way."

Mak brought the jeep to a halt on the rim of the gorge below Big Bench. He looked around for a landmark to tell him where the jeep was left. That stunted cottonwood tree among the boulders in the bed of the gorge would do. Having given up the struggle for life, it spread bleached arms to its Father Sun and waited to die.

Charles Engle alighted, whipped out his binoculars, and trained them on the rugged tableland above. Somewhere up there Jim Barrack was tracking the wild mustang. Gradually he swept the powerful lenses to his right and downward, where the mouths of the canyons yawned, silent and haunted, beyond the front tip of the Bench.

"Is that where we're going to walk, Mak? Way over there?"

"That's where," Mak said. He didn't look up. He filled Engle's canteen from the waterbag on the side of the jeep and handed it to him.

"It won't seem so far, I guess, once we're actually on the way," his companion remarked. "The worst thing is this damned dust that sifts in all around us." He yanked out a tissue to daub at his eyes. "Where does it come from, anyway?" he complained. "There's a dead calm. Not a breath of moving air."

Mak said, "There's always dust in the air deep in Makosica. Don't rub your eyes," he cautioned sharply.

"I have to dig out the dust in order to see anything," Engle retorted.

The oppressive heat, the sense of impending danger, made them touchy over grains of dust.

"A duststorm's on the way, all right," Mak conceded. "It may not hit until tomorrow, though." He clutched at a straw of hope. "Maybe we can reach Spirit Face for a look around and get back home before the wind hits."

Maybe they could . . .

A brief survey around Spirit Face might be enough for Engle to locate fossils — that is, if he was careful not to incur the wrath of the Spirit.

This white man, certainly, had no fear of spirits. He shrugged them off as omens, charms, superstitions. Spirit Face, on the other hand, had nothing to do with white men. Wasn't its power based wholly in Indian legend, Indian religion, Indian land?

Mak began to map their course. "We'll follow the bed of the gorge until it joins the first canyon, which is deeper. The boulders there will be hot and sharp. Watch when you climb over them. We'll by-pass the mouths of the first two canyons. The third one's the place. A giant rock spill makes it a dead end. So we climb the right-hand banks of the gorge. They're like stairsteps. At the top we'll be at the spot where I picked up my wa-sic. Across from Spirit Face."

Coza hadn't the least idea what it cost him even to think about repeating that dreadful journey. He made no attempt to describe the ledge where Shungatoga stood beneath the jutting forehead and cavernous eyes and grinning mouth, spewing out blasts of fire.

He didn't try to tell how he stumbled over his wa-sic in flight. How he found an instant of courage in the small strange bit of power transferred to his pocket, so that he could rope the advancing horse, itself released by wa-sic from the evil grasp of Spirit Face.

He had no words to tell Coza how he fled that awful

171

place with his fearful mission miraculously accomplished.

His wa-sic had come to him to rescue him from the evil spirit. It had not come to take him back there. No Indian wa-sic was that strong.

"Your directions are clear and simple, Mak," Engle said while he poked around in the bed of the jeep. "You make it seem so easy I believe I could find the place by myself. Hold it!" he exclaimed suddenly. "I've forgotten my whiskbroom!" He stared in dismay at Mak over the side of the jeep.

"Then we'll have to get along without it, won't we?" Mak said. A small thing, a forgotten whiskbroom, compared to the mountain of dread that loomed ahead of them.

"But I need that whiskbroom, Mak."

"What for? Didn't you say we find fossils in the open, without having to uncover them?" The way he found his fossil wa-sic.

"I'll need the whiskbroom to brush soil and litter away from the exposed bits," Engle protested. "The way I cleaned out those footprints on Rattlesnake Ridge." He added plaintively, "I don't see small things as well as I might."

"I have good eyes, I can help you on that," Mak offered without softening. He added, "I can use my shirt to swish the dust away."

They looked at one another across the jeep. Mak's face was grim, closed, Engle's distressed, with heat and dust biting into its tender surface.

"Thanks, Mak. Anyway, I want you to drive back to the

bunkhouse and pick up my whiskbroom for me. I left it on my bedstand. Or maybe it's in my duffel bag."

Mak stared as though the forgetful paleontologist had lost his mind as well as his whiskbroom. "But that will take me two hours — there and back."

"It's got to be somewhere in the bunkhouse." Engle frowned at his failure to remember just where. "But then, you can find it for me, Mak. I'll walk on slowly. You can catch up with me before noon."

Engle walk on? He catch up?

What had come over this otherwise reasonable man? Coza behaved like a stubborn kid over a forgotten toy. He would be walking alone in a trackless waste among boulders, beneath a deadly sun, with a windstorm on the way. Coza said at the Council meeting that he had found the message of Makosica. Survival. He should know better than to suggest such a dangerous plan for himself and hope to survive it.

"You said the storm might not hit until tomorrow," Engle argued as though reading Mak's thoughts. "It's still calm. No wind at all." For proof he tested for wind with a tongue-moistened forefinger.

Mak shot Engle a quick glance. Was Coza also testing *him* with silly whiskbroom talk to see if he would chicken out at the last minute? It angered Mak that his employer should offer him this absurd reprieve. Yet all at once relief swept over him like a cool breeze.

Barring a serious fall, Coza could reach the fossil spot within an hour. He had his directions. He couldn't get lost if he stayed in the bottom of the canyon. The storm was

173

hours away. The fossils were there.

"I'll wait for you there, Mak."

Mak nodded, indicating he had heard.

Engle was done with arguing. He barked out sharply, "Don't just stand there. Get going!"

Startled by the harsh tone from his mild-mannered friend, Mak climbed into the jeep. When he hesitated before he stepped on the gas, Coza yelled at him again.

"Go *on!*"

He glared at Mak and threw out his arm in the direction of Barrack Ranch. There was a wildness about him. He looked as though his last chance to succeed with the Foundation had become an insane obsession.

Mak backed the jeep away from the rim of the gorge in a swirl of white dust. Go while he had his last chance, before anything came up to stop him.

Yet, he turned once more to Engle.

"It's at the mouth of the third canyon. Straight ahead."

Engle gave a stiff nod. "You told me."

"Got your snakebite kit?"

"Sure. What do you take me for?"

"How about your compass? Be sure to stay in the bottom of the gully." Mak talked against time. Coza looked so frail and open to attack against the rugged backdrop of Big Bench, the great layers of twisted broken rock upthrust on the gorge floor. The hidden rattlers and thirst-crazed pumas, the evil spirits . . .

"Of course I won't get lost. What a worry-wart you have become, Mak," Engle chided him. He took out his tube of ointment and patted the white salve on his tender nose. "After all the things you have taught me about Makosica,

174

surely I should be able to take care of myself here for an hour or two."

All the things *he* had taught *Coza* about Makosica?

"So long, then."

The jeep lurched away from Engle, who nursed his nose on the rim of the gorge above the dead cottonwood.

Halfway to the ranch a wagon and team of horses appeared out of the suffocating pressure of dust.

At first Mak thought it was a mirage, set in the heat waves by the spirits to frighten him back to Engle.

Then the rickety wagon and mismatched ponies were upon him. The driver lifted his arm in greeting. Mak recognized Adam Redrock in his undented black hat. His plump wife Evangeline sat beside him.

Mak veered to the left to avoid a stop. But it was not the way of Indians to pass on the desert without a greeting.

The Redrock rig halted alongside the jeep. Mak saw a long box made of new wood in the wagon bed behind Adam and Evangeline. A coffin. There had been a death in the Redrock family. Mak knew even before Adam explained. Evangeline's grandfather, Walking Crane, had died in the night. They were taking the old camp crier's body to a final resting place on Happy Hunting Ground Hill beyond Rattlesnake Ridge.

Mak shook his head in sympathy for Evangeline's grief. And partly to clear some question about Walking Crane's death that muddled through his concern over Engle and the whiskbroom.

Adam paused before he lifted the reins to drive on. "What you doin' way out here?"

"I'm guide to the bone man at Barracks'. We forgot his whiskbroom. He needs it to find his fossils. He sent me back for it."

Why trouble to explain his silly errand? Adam Redrock knew nothing about whiskbrooms, or fossils, either. Adam had no idea that he was running away because he was afraid. Even if Adam knew, he would not condemn him. All Indians were afraid of Spirit Face.

"You better stay home when you get there," Adam advised. "A big blow's on the way."

Adam shook the reins and the wagon rolled along with its quiet burden toward Happy Hunting Ground Hill. As it passed, Mak caught sight of a mass of brown feathers stuffed beside the wooden box in the bed of the wagon. Turkey feathers.

The question that nagged him about Walking Crane's death was answered. By sacred custom, Walking Crane took his headdress with him to his Big Sleep. Gail Barrack could not trade her precious pony for it now.

A savage triumph swept through Mak. He turned and sped away home after a forgotten whiskbroom.

25 Encounter in the Bunkhouse

The smoky hush of early morning still blanketed Barrack's dooryard. It muffled Chinook Boy's whinny from the calf pen as the sound of the jeep announced Mak's arrival. The white hens stared motionless and panting from under the cottonwood. Even Yaller failed to rise and bark his noisy welcome. He settled for a drowsy lift of his head to check on Mak's homecoming, then dropped back with a grunt into the shade of the doorstep.

Mak slid the jeep to a quiet halt behind the bunkhouse, rather than in front of it as usual. Just as well that Gail and her parents not know he'd returned. He couldn't take time to explain.

At the threshold of the bunkhouse door his eyes caught sight of the whiskbroom on the table beside Engle's bunk.

Mak stood holding the door open, staring at the whiskbroom, but making no move to take it.

Then there was a scrape of feet and chair legs and Jim Barrack jerked himself out of the rawhide chair behind the open door.

They stood staring at one another.

Jim's face was strained, his heavy brown hair upended from repeated ruffling by nervous fingers.

The night before, each had pledged not to return until he got what he went after.

Mak was first to speak. "Did you — get him?"

"No," Jim answered shortly. "What brought you back here — alone?"

"I came back for Coza's whiskbroom."

"Sure enough?"

Jim Barrack didn't believe him. A reliable Indian guide would not interrupt a deadline fossil hunt in order to return for a whiskbroom. Not with a windstorm brewing.

Mak had to make Jim understand. "It's the way I say, Jim. We headed for the place where I found my wa-sic — Spirit Face, on the canyon wall behind Big Bench. We drove to the gorge as far as the jeep could go. When we got ready to walk the rest of the way, Coza missed his whiskbroom. I said he didn't need it. He wouldn't listen. He said go back and get it. He said he'd go on alone and I could catch up —

"Coza's in a hurry," Mak added, before Jim Barrack's scornful gaze. "He's got to make good with the Foundation before the first of next week."

Jim grasped the whiskbroom from the table and thrust it coldly toward Mak. "Here it is. So what's keeping you?"

Mak looked straight at Jim, his hands at his sides. "Okay, I am scared of Spirit Face. All Indians are scared of it. It's no disgrace."

"But you have your fossil wa-sic to keep you safe," Jim reminded Mak, pushing the whiskbroom at him.

Jim wanted him out of there for another reason. Jim had failed too. That put them on common ground, one no different from the other.

Mak blundered on. "Maybe there's another way to get what we want. I just thought of it. I told Coza how to reach Spirit Face. He knows Makosica good now. He can't get

178

lost in the bottom of the canyon. He's got his compass, his tool pack, his canteen — "

Anger blazed in Jim Barrack's eyes. "You mean you'd leave a tenderfoot like Chuck Engle to find fossils by himself in a desert wilderness? With a storm coming on?"

"Coza yelled at me — he made me come back," Mak countered angrily. "But what I mean is, there's a chance for you and me to get that wild horse and for Coza to find his fossils — both. The windstorm will drive the mustang into a canyon for shelter. It's a good time for us to corner him. I told you it would take two of us to round him up — "

Jim hurled the whiskbroom at Mak's feet. The cords stood out in his muscular neck. For a moment Mak thought Jim meant to take a swing at him.

"I should have known we couldn't trust an Indian guide to carry us through," he blurted out. "You don't care about Chuck. Or about him losing out with the Foundation. You don't care about us losing our ranch, either. You can go live in a cave in the banks of a coulee. You've known all along where those fossils are. But you've let some stupid superstitious hang-up scare you off. You're too much of a coward to face reality and carry through. Even when you're paid to do it. Even when you give your word, and get a decent home out of it besides. First you use a whiskbroom, and now a horse hunt that you don't know anything about, to get out of your bargain."

Jim's big square hands worked at his sides. Mak faced him, stunned by his scornful accusation, his furious eyes.

Then, suddenly Jim stepped back. The surge of his anger began to drain out of him. He drew a deep tight breath.

179

"Okay, Mak, get this. Neither you nor I nor anyone else ever is going to catch that wild mustang. The boys from Cutter Creek got too anxious for that reward. They pushed the stallion too hard, caught him off guard when he was nervous about the storm coming on. They crowded him too close to the east rim of Big Bench and it scared him. Anyway, he led his mares over the edge. Corey Cutter saw the whole thing. From where the herd jumped, Corey said, half the rim of the Bench crumbled off in a rumble of rock and dirt. The mustang is buried with his mares beneath the landslide."

Jim turned to stare out of the bunkhouse window toward Big Bench, hidden now by a rolling bank of dust. "That's why I came home — without what I went after," he said.

Mak stared at Jim's back. Everything was going haywire. The day was dark, though it still wasn't noon. The wild mustang lost in a landslide. Walking Crane's headdress gone forever.

Only the fossils were left.

Mak stood in the darkening bunkhouse, frozen by a thought that scurried like a trapped squirrel through his mind.

"That wild appaloosa mustang," he said slowly, unaware that he was thinking aloud. "He wouldn't be *leading* his mares the way Corey Cutter said. He'd be behind them, circling, sniffing out danger. He'd try to cut out the weak ones, turn the others away from the rim. He wouldn't jump and let himself be caught in a landslide. Not that one. A wild stallion hangs on to life and fights to keep his mares."

Jim Barrack spun quickly from the window. "You

mean to tell me that horse got away?" he demanded. "That he's still alive?" Jim's eyes narrowed. "Is this just some more of your superstitious wish-wash? And you're using it for a last-ditch excuse to promote a horse chase that'll get you out of guiding Chuck Engle to that Spirit Face you're so scared of?"

Jim's charge struck at the core of Mak's being. White men had been felled with tomahawks for less.

Mak realized that Jim Barrack was tortured with facing the loss of his home, his land, his future. Jim didn't know all he was saying. As an Indian Mak might hold an answer that Jim could understand. He made a try.

"What I say is not superstitious wish-wash. Yes, I am Indian. And I know the way of horses. They were put on earth with rights equal to ours. They are a part of us. We honor them. They got us off our feet and moving, to claim all the plainsland of America. You said so yourself."

The quick thought came that he, whose people fought for their Indian homeland, was fighting now beside the usurper to help him hold his own small spot in that same American plainsland.

"What I'm telling you," Mak went on, "is that white men don't know nothing about the way of wild horses compared to us Indians. Not even when it happens in front of their eyes. Those Cutters are only dude ranchers."

Now it was Mak Malloy's face that held the scorn. Jim Barrack ignored it.

"Don't know *anything* about horses," he corrected fiercely. "When will you ever learn to talk *right?*"

Anyway he was right about wild horses, and Jim knew it.

181

Jim looked at him closely, differently, as if he wanted to believe the Indian choreboy was right, the Cutters wrong. That by some streak of luck the wild horse might have escaped the landslide.

He rubbed his hand across his eyes as if to erase something he could have been wrong about for a long time. Something that needed a new look.

They were interrupted by a quick light step in the bunkhouse doorway. Gail Barrack brushed past them. She wore jeans and riding boots, her long hair knotted tightly by a blue scarf.

She sank on the edge of Engle's bunk and looked up at them.

"I heard you two wrangling over the fossils, the whiskbroom, wild horses," she said. "No matter, really, which one is right. I've got the way to settle everything without either your wild horse or your fossils. I'm going to take Paint over to Adam Redrock's place and trade him to Evangeline for Walking Crane's headdress. Then I'll sell my beadwork for whatever it's worth and use the money to see us through the drought. I should have done that in the first place — " She broke off as though suddenly struck by the realization of her lost teacher-dream.

She got to her feet and started out of the door. "I'll ride one of your horses and lead Paint. And don't either of you try to stop me again."

Mak called after her. "You can't have that headdress, Gail, because Walking Crane's — "

Jim shot out of the door, cutting him short.

"You idiot!" he yelled at Gail, holding her. "You can't ride to the reservation now. The windstorm's here. It's already off the Bench — look!"

As he spoke a white hen bounced past them on a gust of wind. Her wings blew out like sails before her as she landed squawking and ruffled in the chokeberry bushes.

The storm struck then with a shrieking roar. It sent a blast of dust rattling against the bunkhouse window. At the barn, a door ripped free of its hinges. Mak watched it twist and bang across the corral, then land in the watering tank.

Gail Barrack would not be stopped. She jerked free of Jim. She threw her arm above her eyes for protection and ran blindly toward the doorless barn to reach the saddle horses.

Jim lunged after her, shouting, grasping for her.

From the bunkhouse doorway Mak watched as they struggled against one another.

The blue scarf sailed away in the scuffle, leaving Gail's long hair whipping about her head like loose straw. She pounded Jim's shoulders with her fists. The way she had pounded on Mak's arm the night before.

Finally, she gave in to her brother's greater strength and the strength of the wind. She clung to Jim's arm sobbing as they started toward the ranchhouse, shrouded in gray dust.

Mak grabbed a denim jacket from a hook for protection against the driving dust. The next moment he slammed the bunkhouse door and groped his way to the jeep.

The engine coughed and shuddered as Mak headed for the gate. He glanced toward Makosica. The hills and escarpments were lost to sight in a solid rolling wall of dust. A single spray of it cut into his cheeks like crumbs of glass.

He'd have to tell Gail later about Walking Crane's lost

headdress. Another thought came to crowd out all others.

Coza was out there in that storm.

With the wind scooping up topsoil from the scorched flats and off the pinnacles, the duststorm soon would envelop the entire badlands country. It suffocated, blinded, confused. A desert duststorm could be as dangerous as any winter blizzard. It *was* a blizzard — a stinging, blinding, fiery black blizzard. Within moments a man could become hopelessly lost in it. Even a man with good eyes . . .

"Mak! Wait, Mak!"

Jim Barrack had pushed his sister safely through the kitchen door. Now he raced, head low, after the jeep, yelling at Mak.

The alarm in Jim's voice, twisted on the wind, gave Mak a fierce satisfaction. Jim sounded like a big brother warning a kid brother against some dreadful danger, determined to meet it with him.

The jeep careened out of Jim's reach. It missed the gatepost, then headed toward the heart of the Makosica.

Jim couldn't help him, anyway. Right now, Jim didn't matter, or the whiskbroom back there on the bunkhouse floor, or the Foundation, or the beadwork. Even the fossils didn't matter.

He had a friend out there in that storm. Coza boasted that he knew Makosica. Coza couldn't see as far as his hand before his face. He couldn't see a rattlesnake coiled inches from his leg. Coza trusted him to come back.

He had to reach him before it was too late.

26 Black Blizzard

A tumbleweed banged into the windshield, making Mak duck. He watched it bounce away to be lost in the clouds of dust, along with the pink peaks, the glistening flats and deep-cut gorges.

He sensed, rather than saw, the shallow banks of the draw that led off the ranch road toward the heart of the badlands. He fumbled at his chest to feel his wa-sic. Moments later he was heading across the desert in the general direction of the gorge and the stunted cottonwood tree that marked the spot where he had left Charles Engle.

Dozens of other such gorges and gullies crisscrossed the windswept wastes, north and south. His only compass was the wind itself. It came at him head-on from the direction of Big Bench.

Gypsum, Engle called the thick white dust that lifted from under the tires to confuse and blind and choke. Wealth it was, tons of it, to harden cement for the dam on the river.

The rim of a gully loomed through the storm. Or could it be the gorge where he had left Engle? Too soon for that.

Yet, as he drove along the gravelly edge, he peered downward through the dust-coated windshield, hopeful for sight of the old tree. It wasn't there, of course.

Mak concentrated on locating the ghostly skeleton of

185

the cottonwood. His eyes ached with the sting of sand. His throat felt stiff and dry. He couldn't take time to drink from his canteen.

The downward slope of the next gully wall tempted him to drive into its sheltered bed. But if boulders should block his way, he might not be able to back the jeep out. Besides, Coza had warned him against leaving the jeep in the bottom of a gully.

Why was Coza so fussy about his jeep? Nothing but a flash flood could harm it in a gully. No flash floods in a duststorm.

Another stretch of flats opened up. The way was easier and in his anxiety to overtake his friend, Mak drove faster. He drove head-on into an outcrop of rock hidden by dust clouds. The sudden halt forced his forehead into the windshield.

Stunned by the impact, Mak's first clear thought was for Engle's jeep. Had he wrecked it? Must he continue the search for Engle afoot?

Coza was right when he boasted that the sturdy little jeep was built like an army tank. It withstood the collision. Mak backed away from the rock obstacle, only to discover that the outcrop was embedded in the edge of another gully. The left rear wheel of the jeep skidded over the rim.

Mak jammed on the brakes. The machine hung sideways over the gully's edge while the wind pushed at it with fiendish force.

Through the swirl of dust Mak caught sight of a mass of boulders in the bed of the gully directly beneath him. To plunge down on the jagged stones could mean death. He clung to the steering wheel of the tottering vehicle. He hardly dared breathe.

Finally he found courage to risk a wrench at the steering wheel. The jeep groaned and lurched. With his body tipped, head downward, Mak managed to feed more gas. The spinning rear wheel gripped solid earth and held. The jeep pulled itself upright, coughed and shuddered, then shot away from the gully's rim like a rabbit freed from a snare.

A long time later Mak skirted the banks of still another gully. His head throbbed with pain from contact with the windshield. His body felt numb with fatigue. Why had he ever believed that he could find Engle in the holocaust that raged across the land? Battered, isolated, he seemed to be heading for something that didn't exist. Something that was etched only in his imagination.

Then he saw it — the old cottonwood on the floor of the gorge immediately beneath him. It beckoned, with frail gray arms, as though it had waited years for him.

Mak left the jeep on the bank above the old tree. He slid down the embankment, the loose stones moving under his feet like marbles. Conglomerate, Engle called it. For the dam. He reached the cottonwood, held to it for a moment, pressing his aching head against the smooth trunk.

Having found his guidepost, he began walking up the bottom of the gorge in the way Engle should have taken over two hours ago — in the direction of the canyon with Spirit Face upon its wall.

The duststorm seemed no less violent in the bed of the gully. Mak yanked his denim jacket above his head and held it tentlike to protect his face against the needles of sand. He worked his way along the stony floor, his thoughts weighted with the fearful certainty of his direction, his eyes straining through the dust for sight of Engle.

The walls of the gorge, eroded by centuries of flash floods, grew higher, the strewn boulders larger and sharper. The stone formations told Mak that he must be entering the first canyon behind Big Bench. He felt the hot suck of a canyon downdraft opposing the straight drive of the wind.

He let out a hoarse shout.

"Coza! . . . Coza?"

When he drew in his breath dust choked him. He washed the grit from his throat with water from his canteen, and called again. And again.

At a bend in the canyon he was stopped short by a pile of great slabs of rock. The angular boulders choked the entire bottom of the gorge. Their great height, their box-like shapes appeared familiar.

Too soon to have reached the third canyon. Yet hadn't he climbed up such a mountain of stone to locate Cloud Rise's lost horse — and found Spirit Face just beyond it?

To avoid the thought, he lowered his eyes from the appalling heights. In front of him two flat slabs of rock came together at a slant, to form a small cave. A lizard, descendant of the mighty dinosaur, scuttled across its entrance.

Exhausted, Mak was unable to resist that tiny pocket of refuge. He sank to his knees and crawled underneath the rocky roof, out of sight of the obstacle of rock and the horror that might be waiting beyond it.

Freed from the whiplash of wind, he huddled in the little cave, his burning face cupped in his hands.

If such a storm could bring him, a strong young Indian, to his knees, what had it done to slight-bodied Charles Engle? If Coza had managed to come this far, he never could have made it over the jagged barrier of rocks.

Mak knew he could not hide. He had to continue his search for Engle, no matter what lay ahead. Yet for another moment, he crouched safely there.

Pain shot through his head in flashes. Vivid, electric-blue flashes they were, like the blowtorch in the machine shop at the Boarding School on the river. The searing ache was followed by a roaring in his head so strong that it shook his body.

He held to his wa-sic, but he couldn't close out the burning flashes, the awful roar. Could the disturbance come from the gorge, outside the cave, and not from his body?

Was this a warning of the spirits, angered by talk of digging bones of strange animals out of Makosica? Talk of hauling away its sacred dust to turn into cement for a dam? Unheard-of talk from Indian people . . .

He lifted his head. The roar and the flashes were gone.

Slowly Mak began to crawl out of the cave. At the entrance he held out his hands to test the dusty air, strangely cool now. The wind had lessened. Two small objects struck his open palms.

They were drops of water.

He stared as more drops came to wet his palms. A current of cool air swept through the gorge. It was followed by a jagged flash of lightning and crash of thunder so loud that it made Mak duck his head.

Then the sky opened up and rain poured down on him in heavy sheets. Even as it came, he couldn't believe.

He leaned against a slab of rock and opened his arms wide as rain came again. And again. He lifted his head and let rain wash away the ache and soothe his dust-stung face and burning eyes. He opened his mouth and drank it and yelled with the joy of it drenching his body.

Rain! . . . A whole rainstorm of it, following the dust-storm, as Engle had predicted.

The long searing misery of drought in Makosica was ended.

At the moment Mak couldn't think of all that the end of drought meant to him. He was consumed by the sweet scent and sound of the rain, washing the air clean of dust and heat. It dashed off the boulders, spattered on the ground at his feet. It was like the pound of drums, dancing feet, and the songs of all the nations of his race. The blazing blue crackle of lightning and roar of thunder became beautiful music. No longer the threat of evil spirits.

A sheet of lightning highlighted a shadowy movement to the right of him. A horse was climbing up the boulders in the middle of the canyon. It lunged and stumbled and strained its body through the rain to reach the top of the rocks.

A ghost horse, behind the shimmering curtain of silver . . .

The horse had black spots that mottled its body, a black mane and tail. It was not a ghost at all, but real, alive. An appaloosa! Mak stared, hardly believing what he saw. That horse, scrambling frantically up the rocks through the rain, had to be the wild appaloosa mustang stallion from Big

Bench! No other such horse anywhere around.

As Mak watched, the wild appaloosa reached the top slab of rock, swiveled, lowered his head, and hunched his spotted rump against the storm, to wait it out.

So he had been right after all. The wild horse *was* too smart to run into danger ahead of his skittish mares. He had saved himself and probably some of his mares, by veering instinctively away from the cumbling point of the Bench. As the landslide broke away, he had evaded the Cutter boys through the cloud of rising dust, then escaped down the opposite side of the Bench into the gorge. The windstorm had overtaken him in the upper canyon.

Mak thought, staring at the hunched, rain-drenched animal, "I could have him for Jim if I'd gone back for my rope instead of that stupid whiskbroom."

As it was, when the storm cleared, the appaloosa would be gone, lost once more in the vast reaches of Big Bench.

A high-pitched quavering voice came from beyond the mountain of rocks. A coyote, he thought, its lone howl coming faintly through the downpour. Yet, it didn't sound like the voice of the song dog.

Mak forgot the horse, the danger of the sharp rocks. He began to climb, to locate the strange-echoing voice. Halfway up the rocky mound he straightened and looked across the tilted boulders.

Through the rain and flashes of lightning he saw something move along the ledge of a canyon wall ahead of him. The position of the canyon and its ledge held no meaning for him then. All his attention was fixed on that figure, moving behind the sheet of rain.

Not the song dog. Hardly human, either, with its

scrawny neck and arms, and short flapping rag of garment. Drenched, gesturing in a kind of excited danger-dance, the figure seemed to be a living mixture of stone-picture and cartoon torn from one of Mary's comic sheets.

While Mak stared through the rain, the howling apparition continued to beckon wildly.

Then Mak knew.

That red-faced, wild-looking being over there on the canyon ledge, screaming and waving his arms in the rain, was Coza!

27 Find at Spirit Face

Mak stared at Coza from across the rain-lashed boulders.

Coza had weathered the duststorm. He had climbed across that mountainous hodgepodge of rocks and reached the ledge, out of the storm.

By some vagary in the wind, Coza had heard his dust-choked call from the canyon far below. Coza's answer, twisted and quavering through the howling storm, finally had caught his ears.

Now he stood there, a long stone's throw away, yelling and motioning, as though to warn Mak of some danger.

His frantic words came muffled through the thunderous downpour like the whining buzz of a horsefly.

Finally, Mak heard a still louder roar above that of the rain. It was like no sound he'd ever heard before. Out of the rising din, he saw a wall of brown water lift beyond the ledge where Engle stood pointing. It began to rush past Engle from the canyon above him. It looked like the brown backs of a thousand stampeding buffalo —

Mak knew about flash floods in Makosica. Swift to come, briefly terrible, then gone. He should know about the canyon, too, that ledge, the piled boulders. No time to think it through now.

Time only to realize that he stood directly in the path of the floodwaters pouring from the canyon above. And that Engle warned him to get out before he was dashed to death on the rocks.

Instinctively Mak headed for the nearest bank, scrambling hurriedly over the slippery tilted rocks. They sloped upward, toward the canyon rim, which was an advantage. Yet, already the floodwaters, seeking their level, formed a narrow river rushing through a pocketlike crevice between himself and the rim of the bank. In seconds, the wall of water from the canyon would engulf all but the highest rocks in the canyon and overflow the banks.

The wild appaloosa had sensed this. He stood securely on his pinnacle beyond Mak, and gazed down at the on-coming flood.

Already the water lapped at Mak's ankles as he hurried over sharp hidden edges and slippery surfaces. He strained to hold his balance against the force of water that pushed at his feet, then at the calves of his legs. He couldn't see or feel anything but water. It beat on his body from the sky and pulled at his legs on the rocks.

Water that he had prayed for these long months — that he had welcomed as a lifesaver only moments ago — now would destroy him. A narrow raging river rushed between him and the banks of the canyon.

A queer long object, shining like pink china, reached toward him over the narrow, swirling waters.

Mak blinked.

What *was* that thing? It looked like an arm . . . Coza's arm!

The ledge where Engle had stood sloped downward from the canyon wall to meet with the banks of the canyon. No matter how he remembered. From his Dream, maybe —

Anyway, Coza had rushed down the incline to throw himself on the bank opposite him. His prone body already was partly submerged as he reached out. Mak heard his faint, gasping shout.

"Jump, Mak!"

In seconds Coza would be washed away, drowned in the water rising over the banks. What did a geology professor know about the danger of jumping into a torrent of water raging over sharp hidden rocks? What kind of help lay in that skinny pink arm stretched out to him?

No choice. The wall of floodwater from the canyon above struck the piled rocks. A monster wave swept Mak off his feet. He was tossed like a leaf into the whirlpool.

A knife-edge of rock scraped the skin of his thigh as he fell. A jab into his ribs made him lose his breath. His foot found a hold in an embedded rock to stay him briefly against the force of the current.

He caught a swift glimpse of Engle's face upstream, glasses awry on his sunburned nose. Too far away to help him.

Engle flipped over like a fish in an effort to come closer. His arm shot out again, slapping the water to catch Mak's attention.

Mak lost his foothold on the rock. He was pulled under in the raging crevice just as he gripped the outstretched hand.

Engle pulled. *Mak hadn't thought that Coza was so strong!*

Then Charles Engle dragged him, choked and floundering, over the rim of the canyon.

They stood in the water that overflowed the banks, held to one another for a moment, gasping, unable to move. Finally they waded and stumbled and splashed up the incline to the ledge. They halted under a rocky overhang out of the reach of flood and rain.

Across the way, the wild horse stood like a statue on an island in the middle of a swollen river.

"I — I thought you'd never get here, Mak."

"I never could've made it without you," Mak gasped. What could he say to this limp drenched man who had saved him from drowning? "I forgot your whiskbroom," he said.

"We don't need it after all," Engle assured him with shaky cheer. "We can't use a whiskbroom in mud, can we, Mak!"

They laughed together in choking gasps, like boys turned silly after a scare.

Engle looked away from the angry rush of brown water at his feet as though to get it out of sight and mind. From force of habit he began to scan the canyon wall opposite him for fossils. Its wet sides shone like bronze through the falling rain. "I never should have sent you back for it in the first place," he said, adjusting his crooked glasses for clearer vision. "I worried about you all the time you were gone."

Engle, worried about *him?*

"Just as well I went back, because I found — " What *had* he found on his return to the bunkhouse? Besides the whiskbroom. An angry understanding with Jim Barrack. The death of an old Indian that halted Gail Barrack's sacrifice to hold her home. A part of himself he'd found there, too, all mixed up with wild horses and fossils and a helpless lost friend.

"I guess I found out that I could remember not to park the jeep in the bed of a gully," he answered Engle with a wet-faced grin. "Good thing you kept reminding me. It would be swept away by now."

Engle nodded absently. His jeep was of little importance at the moment. He squinted at the canyon wall across the moving body of muddy water. His thin torso still heaved beneath the rag of shirt plastered against it.

"Let's get down to business, Mak. Do you see what I see on that rock wall across the way from us?"

The crashes of thunder and lightning had lessened. The cloudburst settled into a steady downpour. Engle pointed through it. "I mean that curved layer of rock that bulges out over the strata halfway up on the side of the canyon," he said.

"I see it. What about it? That's just a part of the wall. Sandstone."

"Right," agreed Engle, "except for the part that curves out. That isn't sandstone. I'm disappointed in you, Mak," he added as Mak hesitated, "after all I've taught you about rocks."

Mak caught a thread of excitement running through Engle's mild scolding that was vaguely familiar.

"Hey!" he exclaimed. "That curve of stone is lighter than the strata above it. So it's limestone. That's a fossil up there!" he declared. "A long one — part of a backbone." He broke off to stare at Engle. "Could that be the backbone of some, some . . ."

"That could be the backbone of some prehistoric animal, all right," Engle agreed, pleased at Mak's recognition of it. "A mastodon, if I see it correctly. It stands out plain as day now that the rain has washed it clean. You can see where the ribs begin. Set in the curved backbone that way, they look like teeth. In some ungodly grin. In fact, together the backbone and the battered ribs make a mouth in a face. If you look farther up and use your imagination . . ."

Mak didn't need to use his imagination. He couldn't take his eyes from the reality of the face in the rock of the canyon wall — the two caverns above the grin, the perpendicular overhang that made the nose . . .

"Eyes, nose, mouth — a whole face. See it, Mak?"

"Of course I see it. Stop talking, Coza. *Stop it.* Until I think . . ."

The rock-bloated canyon, the sloping ledge, the face — all came together in his mind like the pieces in a puzzle. Now he realized where he was standing. The grisly face that this excited white man pointed to, already was well known to him, and to hundreds of Indian people.

It was Spirit Face!

His first thought was to run away through the rain. But he couldn't seem to move from beside Engle. The shock of his discovery had dulled his senses, locked his muscles.

Engle slapped his shoulder under the soggy denim jacket. "Mak, we've made our fossil find! Right out in the open. Better than anything we ever imagined!"

Mak nodded, eyes glued to the opposite wall. Wet, shiny with rain, Spirit Face looked different. The evil grin had changed into a smile, the frowning features beaming, benign.

But he musn't be fooled. Spirit Face was evil, terrible, just as the legend had it. Ready to destroy him any minute.

Engle's jubilant voice droned in his ear. "An entire mastodon's got to be buried there in that wall, Mak. The Foundation will go for this find in a big way. I'll rig up a temporary platform on the wall, get some samples, make some measurements, and recommend they send out a digging expedition at once. With headquarters at Barracks' Ranch . . ."

Just like that. The expedition and the rain would help the Barracks to keep their ranch. A whole family together again, belonging, secure in their land, in their work.

But first he had to reckon with Spirit Face. He couldn't think, with Engle babbling about rigging, picks, and drills.

"We can get a good start on this dig before the snow flies, Mak. If it is a bad winter we'll take a break until spring. By next summer we can go at the dig in earnest. You'll be home from school then to work right with us."

Who said anything about school? He was done with books and classrooms, wasn't he? Right now there was this thing between himself and Spirit Face to get straight.

"When this fellow died, his body finally became buried with tons of sand." Stimulated by his discovery, Engle's agile mind receded into the dark ages. "Pressures turned the sand into layers of stone — the skeleton itself into stone. The body's been held in the strata of this wall until centuries of flash floods like this one eroded it and brought the backbone and ribs to the surface for us to find."

Stuff I already know, Mak though impatiently. Engle's enthusiasm blocked his disordered thoughts, kept him from understanding about the change in Spirit Face, his own strangely changed feeling about it.

"There probably are pieces from this mastodon fossil scattered everywhere below this ledge," Engle predicted.

Mak clutched his wa-sic on its string. Finding security there, he groped his way back to the beginning. "I already found one of the pieces. My wa-sic," he said. "It was the day I trailed Cloud Rise's lost horse through the canyon and roped him here. Just below this ledge. Where you pulled me out. My wa-sic and my Dream said the fossils were here. I already told you that the spirits make it a dangerous place. It's Spirit Face."

Now it was Engle who stared, first at the face on the wall, then at Mak. "Of course, Mak, that's got to be Spirit Face up there. And this surely *is* a dangerous place. I'm scared of it, too."

"All Indians are. That's why I couldn't guide you here. I guess I told you all that, too."

Characteristically Engle brushed aside repetition and

emotional stress in order to probe the heart of the matter. "How about now?"

"I don't know. I'm just not scared of it anymore." Mak answered slowly, staring up at the face on the wall. "To look at it, sort of gets me." He cupped his hand above his heart in the sign to express feeling. "But it doesn't scare me anymore."

Charles Engle recalled how Mak had sided with him, a white man, who questioned the sacred beliefs of his ancestors in order to bring a new understanding of their sacred wasted desert. Beliefs deeply ingrained in the young Indian's being.

A scientist, Engle did not back away from facts. He said quietly, "Fear, for the most part, is a thing of the mind, Mak. Give it a place and it stays. Given half a chance, it leaves. You have given it half a chance."

But how? What chance had he taken against his sacred birthright? Except to listen, to read, to seek to know his own Earth Mother better. So that now, by the miracle of change, when he came to stand unknowingly before the dreaded Spirit Face, he no longer saw it as an evil spirit. He saw it as a fossil.

Could Spirit Face be divided, then, like himself, part spirit, part fossil?

"Don't try to figure it out now," Engle advised, noting the confusion in Mak's face. "You won't be able to figure this thing through all at once. Takes time."

Mary said it took time to change. Suddenly Mak had a childish longing to be with Mary again . . .

Beside him, Engle fumbled at the neck of his shirt.

"It's still there, Mak," he exclaimed in smiling surprise.

"What's still there?"

"You haven't listened to a word I said," Engle complained. "I mean my wa-sic, my rhino's tooth. After all I've gone through today, my rhino's tooth still is around my neck! But not gnawing at me anymore," he added soberly.

Mak gave a faint grin. Coza had said that all men had their superstitions. This incredible man, who had brought him out of yesterday into today, now took him back to his beginnings.

"Why wouldn't it still be there, Coza? That was what brought you to find this fossil face, wasn't it — your wa-sic, gnawing?"

"My wa-sic and yours together," Engle amended. "Neither of us had wa-sic strong enough to make it alone." He gave Mak a little push. "So let's let our wa-sic take us back to the jeep and start us off to tell the good news to the Barracks."

They turned from the fossil face on the canyon wall and started down the slope of the ledge through the rain. It would be a rough trip, wading, skirting gushing gullies, crossing gypsum flats that had become shallow lakes.

But then, as Engle declared, they had strong wa-sic to take them through.

28 Another Beginning

The storm was over. Huge clouds flared out and sailed above the pink peaks and tabletops, and washed flats. Their crisp fluff brought a new quality of resistance to the land, bathed of drought and springing to belated summer bloom.

Mak breathed it all in, wanting to make a song about it. He couldn't find the words. His heart was too full. So were the hearts of the Barracks.

They had listened under the cottonwood while Mak and Coza told of the search through the duststorm, the rescue from the flash flood, the unexpected appearance of the wild horse. And finally, the discovery of Spirit Face as a fossilized prehistoric skeleton embedded in the upper canyon wall.

Jim had to see for himself. "Drive me over there, Mak. I want to take a look at that fossil face. I've got to check out that wild horse, too, while the sand's still wet enough to hold his tracks."

So now they stood together on the ledge below Spirit Face. As expected, the waters of the flash flood had receded to a narrow rushing trickle along the right-hand embankment. The vast heap of rocks, submerged in yesterday's floodwaters, already were dry in the early morning sun. The pinnacle rock, where the horse had stood, towered above the others like an empty throne.

"We'll trail him in a minute," Jim said. He jerked his eyes from the vacant site to look more closely at Spirit Face. Bathed in sunshine, it stood out of the canyon wall like some crude and massive painting, not quite dry from the artist's brush.

Jim's scrutiny moved up the rocky wall, studying the cavernous eyes between the perpendicular overhang, the jagged, toothy curve of the fossilized backbone.

"Easy to understand why you Indians call it Spirit Face," he said, awed by the mammoth rock image. "And why you'd be scared of it."

Jim's words were brief apology for his accusation of Mak's fear. He didn't expect Mak to explain the meaning of Spirit Face, or his earlier fear of it. Following their quarrel in the bunkhouse Jim had come to understand that no white man held the right to question the sanctities of the Indian heart. He let the matter drop.

"After Chuck Engle and his crew get a crack at it," he added thoughtfully, "Spirit Face will be gone. Nothing will be left to scare an Indian again."

Mak had been wondering about that. How would his people take the loss of Spirit Face? True, in their excited prospect over a new dam to relieve their suffering crops, they had voted permission for Engle to dig fossils any-where in Makosica. Thought of Engle digging Spirit Face out of the canyon wall was farthest from their minds. Fearful as it was, Spirit Face was a part of their legendary religious belief.

As Mak stared at Spirit Face with conflicting thoughts, a small bird exploded out of nowhere. It perched on one of the jagged, toothlike rib bones that formed the giant mouth.

The bird began to sing in joyful, full-throated notes. Out of the scattered echoes of its song, Spirit Face seemed to be intoning the words Mary had spoken at the Council meeting.

. . . the scars of change will be healed by wind and rain . . . while we change our way of life, we can still keep ourselves Indian at heart . . .

The bird flew away, leaving only a dying echo of its song.

Mary's words had readied her people for acceptance of this final change. The bird gave the sign. They stony image of Spirit Face must go, along with the buffalo, to remain only in their memories.

"Let's get on with tracking that wild appaloosa," Jim said.

They found hoof prints farther on, below the canyon wall where it skirted the base of Big Bench.

"Five mares and two colts — besides the stallion," Mak decided after a close examination of the trampled patch of damp sand. "The mares joined him here about sunrise, when the flood went down."

"So where are they now?" Jim asked.

"They probably returned to Big Bench. They could make the climb at the point this side of the landslide."

The bodies of the remainder of the herd almost certainly lay beneath the landslide. "That puts us back at another beginning," Jim said after a moment. He looked at Mak. "How do we go about tracking him down?"

It was easier now for Jim to ask advice and help from

an Indian. Easy to expect to accomplish the job together.

Mak answered out of a long, carefully considered plan. "There's a dead-end canyon on the back side of the Bench with a hidden spring. The stallion's cagey about hanging around there and he won't have to, now that he can drink from puddles. But in a week or two, when the puddles dry up, he'll lead his mares back there. We can rock up the mouth of the canyon, then throw up a corral and break him there. When he's ready, we can lead him home."

Jim grinned. "Sounds simple, the way you put it."

"It'll take time." Mak didn't want Jim to think that he knew everything about bringing in a wild horse. "It'll take both of us."

"We have all the time we need," Jim said. "No other riders will horn in on us, because the Cutter boys are telling around that the whole herd died under the landslide. We sure can use the five mares and the colts, too," he added.

"Right."

Jim needled Mak good-naturedly. "After we break the stallion, I'm banking on your wa-sic to help him call his mares to our pasture gate to start breeding my appaloosa herd. Right?"

"With a little rope help from you and me," Mak grinned.

"It's a deal, pard." Jim looped his arm over Mak's shoulder and they started toward the jeep.

As Jim said, they were back at a new beginning.

It was late June when Mak helped Engle rig a scaffold and chip samples of fossil from Spirit Face for examination by fellow scientists at the Foundation.

Before Engle left the ranch to organize his expedition, Mak drove Mary's nephew, Joseph Blackstone, and Emil Berry, the Agency clerk, to Rattlesnake Ridge. They took samples of gravel for the new dam from the coulee below the remains of the prehistoric land turtle. They explored another gravel site at Indian Rock, where the puma had died.

Emil Berry supported a pad on his bended knee to make notes while Joseph Blackstone tested for gypsum at Scorpion Flats, still muddy from rain.

"Right now the flats look more like a buffalo wallow than a mine of minerals." Joseph grinned from beneath his red windband.

"If winter holds off, we should begin hauling gravel for the dam by the first of October," Emil Berry told Engle. "Already the government has given Superintendent Stoner the go-ahead to buy two gravel trucks and a shovel." He added, "We've been swamped with applications for truck drivers from the younger Indians. Among them, Les Bentarm."

Mak said dryly, "Les will do okay as a trucker — once he gets on to the difference between handling a motorcycle and a gravel truck."

The Barrack family gathered in the dooryard to see Engle and his samples off to his college. Mr. Barrack stepped into the ranch pickup ready to drive him to the airport in Great Falls.

Yaller circled the pickup in a frenzy, while Mak helped load the last of Engle's books and fossil artifacts.

"I hear that Whitehorn High is offering a course in

206

geology this coming fall," Engle remarked casually to Mak.

"Yeah." Mak grinned. So Gail had been talking, taking a lot for granted. The description of the geology course and the girl's enthusiastic plans for them to board with Aunt Martha had edged him into considering a year in town at the white man's school.

"It's in the bag, Chuck," Gail said happily, now that Mak had committed himself. "And thanks for leaving us the jeep. It'll get Mak and me back to the ranch from Aunt Martha's for weekends."

Charles Engle shook hands all around. "Be sure you and Mak get that appaloosa finished off before I come back," he warned Jim. "You can't have Mak after I return with the expedition in September. That gives you two months. I've hired Mak to work weekends with us this fall at Spirit Face."

"Then who's going to chop my kindling?" Mrs. Barrack wanted to know.

"You've chopped your own kindling, Polly, long before Mak came to live with us," Mr. Barrack teased his wife from behind the steering wheel of the pickup. "I'll be around to sub for Mak," he assured her, "while I ready quarters for the expedition. And feed and water Chinook Boy. And start ploughing for another stand of wheat."

Good to feel needed, Mak thought; good to be busy, sharing the work, looking ahead together.

The engine of the pickup roared. They waved Charles Engle off.

"Be seeing you, Coza," Mak yelled after him. "Don't take no wooden nickels," he added, the way the truckers had called back when pulling away from Halfway House.

Jim scowled at him as the pickup disappeared down the ranch road. "I hope that geology teacher works your grammar over good while he teaches you what you don't already know about rocks."

29 The Last Piece

It was a warm weekend early in Moon of First Frost. Leader, the subdued appaloosa mustang stallion, watched from his new box stall while Jim gentled the last of his five mares at the snubbing post.

In another week Engle and his work force would arrive to dismantle Spirit Face.

A letter came from Pop in California, and Mak drove to Antelope, at the east edge of Makosica, to show the letter to Mary. Talk it over. Visit together like old times. There was much to tell her.

He found Mary bent over beadwork in the leaf arbor behind her sister's cabin, chewing her coffee bean. Her graying hair hung in smooth braids over her breast. Her sister's newest baby lay asleep in her lap. Now and then Mary interrupted her work to move a hand, fanlike, above the infant's face to ward off a fly.

The other children screamed around a mudhole in the draw below them. They hadn't heard the arrival of the jeep. Mak recognized the sharp yapping of Mary's mongrel dog above the din.

A smile broke over Mary's broad face when his shadow fell before her.

He squatted, Indian fashion, and held out the letter. "From Pop," he said. "Just came."

"You read it," Mary said. "My eyes are not so good anymore."

Mary never had read well. Her rendition of the funnies in the kitchen at Halfway House had been a garbled mixture of English and Indian words, highly colored with native imagination.

Pop's scribble told of a well-deserved life of ease at his brother's home in California. Eating prunes off a tree, mind you, wading in the warm ocean, driving a new car to visit missions, parks, the zoo. Come to California and I'll show you the sights, Pop wrote. He enclosed a bus ticket.

Mary looked up anxiously. "You go?"

"Just for Christmas," Mak answered. "It's a two-way ticket. Pop knows I've got to get back to finish school with Gail in Whitehorn. And to work with Coza weekends on the fossil dig at Spirit Face beginning soon."

"Spirit Face? Fossil dig?" she repeated.

He told her how wa-sic had led Engle and himself to the great fossil on the canyon wall that made up the features of Spirit Face. He explained it simply, in full, without pause.

"I'm not scared of it anymore, because I know that it was not left there by the spirits. It's made of fossilized bones of one of the great prehistoric animals that Coza told about at the Council meeting. Fierce changes that split our Mother, the Earth, and flash floods that wore it down, finally brought it out for us to see, and know the truth. Its fire-breath was only a downdraft in the canyon. Before long Coza's workmen will dig Spirit Face off the canyon wall. And it will be no more. We gave Coza a permit to do that," Mak reminded her. "Pieces of the animal's skeleton will be shipped to a museum and hooked together so everybody can look at it. And learn."

Mary recalled the story. If she was disturbed by the unexpected profaning of their legend's fearful spirit creature, she did not show it. She looked out over Makosica, her moving hand seeming to brush such thoughts aside along with the flies.

Their great and terrible land. Part of it created by upthrust, all of it carved and remolded by devil winds and torrential water. Its pale drab flats were tinged now with a green fuzz of new cactus and sage sprouted by the rain. Already Father Sun, a fierce, unrelenting god, was regaining his domination over the land. By next spring blazing heat and scouring wind would bring sweat and dust to men digging around a government truck out there. But Mary and Mak knew that the earth the workmen scratched with their shovels would move slowly back into a destiny of its own.

His deserted boyhood cave-haunt already had receded into the banks of the coulee, Mak had noted as he drove past it. A mat of tumbleweeds sealed its mouth to preserve the pictographs, the scent of damp earth and dead fires left by his ancestral Earth People.

"Miss Gail, does she wear the moccasins?" Mary asked finally, without turning.

He smiled. "Yes, unless she walks barefoot, or wears riding boots."

He knew Mary was fond of the ranch girl who had purchased the beadwork that Indian women sold to help them through hard times. "Gail plans to be a teacher some day when the schoolhouse is built on the school section," he informed Mary. "She plans to sell her collection of our women's beadwork to pay her way through teacher's college. After she finds one more last piece, that is."

Mary asked after a moment, "You go to this college with Miss Gail then?"

Mak shook his head. "No. I'll finish Whitehorn High, then stay on at Barrack Ranch, work with fossils for Coza. Help Jim break horses. Do chores."

Mary shifted the sleeping baby on her knee to reach into the pocket of her full, blue percale skirt. She brought out a small flat book and handed it to Mak.

He saw that it was her savings book with the Whitehorn bank.

"I want that you should go to this college, too," she said, "like Joseph and Mr. Jim and Miss Gail. A long time I saved my money for that. You will help Makosica better, when you come back from that college school."

Mak looked at the tiny worn book, filled with faint columns of figures. He thought of the years Mary had cooked for truckers and tourists in Pop's hot little lean-to kitchen.

The countless beads she sewed on buckskin in order to realize her hopes for him.

Coza had said that college was not for all. Yet, wasn't it Coza's fund of knowledge about rocks, Coza's fascinating college books, that helped him to find work and a home in Makosica?

He thought of Gail Barrack's eager eyes as she read aloud the folder about the geology course. He was nagged once more with the thought that she was only a year older than he, yet she knew so much more.

And there was Joseph Blackstone, who went to college to learn how to build dams to improve the lives of his fellow tribesmen. As Pop said, he did not have to come back like the others, like Les Bentarm and Wings. Maybe he'd learn to talk right at college too.

He couldn't tell Mary how he felt about all this now — the savings book in his hands, the college thing.

"Thank you, my Mother," he said.

"Makosica, the Earth, is your Mother," she reminded him fiercely.

He answered as fiercely, "I will not forget that again."

His Mother ... she gave him choices between sacred beliefs and proven facts. Bound him securely in her blanket of certain change, her deep violent struggle, her beauty, her worth. All his needs as Indian were found on her mighty bosom, Mary told them at the Council meeting.

Mak's heart was too full for more talk. He got to his feet to make his leave.

"Wait," Mary said.

She laid the sleeping child on a deerskin mat and disappeared into her sister's cabin. In a moment she returned with a long, battered cardboard carton, blowing the dust from its cover.

Mak recognized it as the box that held Mary's most prized possession — her great-grandfather Earth Boy's chieftain headdress.

"You take this to Miss Gail for the last piece," she told him in the mother tongue. "Tell her there is good wa-sic in it from the great chief who wore it. Tell her its power can wipe out old fears and hates for our young ones the way Bone Man wipes Spirit Face off the canyon wall." She added, contradicting the even tone of her voice with a strain of native defiance, "We old ones never can change all our ways. That's good, because then we are able to pass on some of our old ways that keep our young ones strong in finding new ways."

Having shown her loyalty to her origins, Mary qualified it in the name of the sleeping baby. "We can't have our young ones grow up like those great animals that died out, so our bone men say, because they couldn't change. You tell Miss Gail that."

"I'll tell Miss Gail," Mak promised, smiling with her across the great chieftain's headdress.

She looked at him, this strong, serious white man's orphaned child whom she had carried across Makosica on her blanketed back. Fast changing now into a man.

Her eyes lingered on the bit of fossil hanging above his heart. "You hold to wa-sic?" she asked. She knew, but she wanted to hear him say it.

"Always," he answered her. "Its power came from my Earth Mother to make me a man, and to keep me Indian in my own land."

"Wasta." Satisfied, Mary turned from him to gather up the sleeping baby.

Mak drove away through a flaming sunset to take Chief Earth Boy's headdress home to Gail Barrack.

The long wailing notes of Mary's sundown prayer song floated after him.